HELP!

I'M TRAPPED IN A
MOVIE STAR'S BODY

Other books by Todd Strasser

HELP!
I'M TRAPPED IN A MOVIE STAR'S BODY

TODD STRASSER

AN
APPLE
PAPERBACK

SCHOLASTIC INC.
New York Toronto London Auckland Sydney
Mexico City New Delhi Hong Kong

ISBN 0-590-97803-9

12 11 10 9 8 7 6 5 4 3 2   8 9/9 0 1 2 3/0

Printed in the U.S.A.   40

First Scholastic printing, October 1998

*To Lisa Callamaro —
who knows what
it's like.*

1

"**H**ere goes, guys," I said. "A reverse spinning fadeaway layup."

My friends Josh Hopka and Andy Kent glanced at each other and rolled their eyes in disbelief. We were playing horse before school started.

"A *fadeaway* layup?" Josh said with a smirk. "That's impossible."

"Seeing is believing." I drove to the basket and launched the shot.

"I don't believe it!" Andy snorted when the ball dropped in.

"Hey, guys, guess what?" Alex Silver yelled as he ran onto the basketball court. Alex was sometimes our friend and sometimes too cool to be our friend.

"Jake made an impossible shot," Josh said.

"No, something else," said Alex. "You'll never believe it."

My friends and I immediately accepted the challenge.

"The hummingbird is the only warm-blooded animal that can fly backward?" Josh guessed.

"No," said Alex.

"They've figured out why noses run and feet smell?" guessed Andy.

"Nope," replied Alex.

"The cannibal wouldn't eat the clown because it tasted funny?" I guessed.

Alex gave me a puzzled look. "What?"

"Forget it," Josh said. "So what's up?"

"They're making a movie here in Jeffersonville," Alex announced excitedly.

"Who is?" Josh asked.

"The company that made the *Screech* movies," Alex said.

The *Screech* movies were a series of horror flicks that starred a handsome teenage heartthrob named Erie Lake. The trademark of each movie was the moment when Erie found himself covered from head to foot by disgusting creepy crawly creatures.

"Why would they make a movie here in Jeffersonville?" Andy asked.

"Nobody knows," Alex answered. "But Julia Sax talked to someone from the movie company yesterday."

"So?" Josh asked.

Alex looked surprised. "Don't you think it's incredibly cool?"

"It's not like we're gonna be in it or anything," Andy said.

"Yeah," agreed Josh. "They always use professional actors. And they'll probably have security guards to keep us from getting too close."

"He's right, Alex," I said. "It sounds really cool at first, but when you think about it, it's just a big 'so *what?*'"

Alex's shoulders sagged with disappointment. "Gee, I never thought of it that way."

Briiiinnng! From Burp It Up Middle School came the sound of the morning bell.

"I hate to burst your bubble, Alex," I said as we headed into school. "But none of us are going to get rich and famous."

2

My friends and I didn't think the movie was a big deal, but the rest of the school sure did. Kids were talking about it in their classes. Between periods, teachers met in the halls and whispered excitedly.

At lunch in the cafetorium, kids at every table were talking about Erie Lake and the movie.

"What are they all so excited about?" Josh asked as we ate.

"Yeah," scoffed Andy. "It's just a dumb movie."

Amber Sweeny put her tray down a few seats away from us. Amber was the prettiest girl and the smartest kid in our grade. "Did you hear the latest?" she asked. "They're going to use kids from our school as extras."

"Extra what?" Andy asked.

"Extras in the movie, silly," Amber said. "For scenes where they need a crowd of kids to walk down a hall or run away from some huge monster."

"Kids from *our* school?" Andy's jaw fell.

"No way!" argued Josh.

"Yes, way," replied Amber. "Amanda Gluck's mom works for the *Jeffersonville Examiner*. She says the movie company called this morning and placed a big ad for extras."

Josh and Andy turned to each other and cried, "We're gonna be famous!"

3

My friends jumped to their feet and started dancing around, giving one another high fives and singing:

"Oh, yeah, it's groovy, we're gonna be in a movie!
Like wow, it's cool, we'll never come back to school!
Like totally, for sure, I'm gonna get a manicure!
The sun, I swear, it better bleach my hair!
Go, go! Fight, fight! Boy, I hope I look all right!
Groovy, cool, what a scene! We'll be in every magazine!"

"Uh, guys?" I tried to interrupt, but Josh and Andy were too busy celebrating to hear me.

"Guys?" I said, louder. But they still didn't hear me.

"HEY, MEATHEADS!" I shouted.

Josh and Andy stopped dancing. "What?"

"I thought you didn't care about the movie," I said.

"That was *before* we found out we could be in it," Andy explained.

"Yeah," Josh agreed. "Now it's the coolest thing *ever!*"

"A limo!" exclaimed Andy.

"A private jet!" added Josh.

"A swimming pool!" Andy said.

"An entourage!" Josh cried.

Andy and I both stared at him. "A *what?*"

"Don't you guys know what an entourage is?" Josh asked.

Andy and I shook our heads.

"Every star has one," Josh explained. "Haven't you ever read in a magazine about so-and-so and his entourage?"

"So what is it?" I asked.

Josh shrugged. "I was hoping one of you guys would know."

"Maybe it's something you wear," I guessed.

"Or a pet," Andy guessed. "You know how stars always have weird pets. I bet an entourage is some kind of dog. Like from France."

"So we'll get entourages!" Josh cried gleefully.

Slap! Andy and Josh shared another high five.

"Wait a minute," I said. "They're only looking for extras. Extras don't get to act. They don't

7

even have lines. They're just part of the crowd."

"But it's a *start*!" Andy replied.

"Yeah," Josh chimed in. "That's just the beginning. First you're an extra, and then pretty soon you're doing TV shows."

"And then TV movies," said Andy.

"And then your own sitcom," said Josh.

"And then *real* movies," said Andy.

"And then what?" I asked.

Andy made a face like the answer was totally obvious. "Then you're famous, dummy."

"And rich," added Josh.

"A millionaire!" said Andy.

"*A billionaire!*" cried Josh.

They started to dance and sing again:

"Oh, yeah, it's cool, we'll never go back to school!
We're hot, we're tight, we'll be out every night!
A pool, a jet, a French entourage.
A beach house, a mansion, a twelve-car garage!
A Porsche, a Benz, a red Ferrari.
If you're not our friend, you'll really be sorry!"

"Calm down, boys." It was Principal Blanco, and with him were two people we'd never seen before. One was a tall woman wearing a black jacket and matching pants. Her black hair was pulled back tightly in a bun, and she was wearing

8

sunglasses. The other was a man wearing a bright yellow-and-blue Hawaiian shirt and white slacks. He had short blond hair. A camera was hanging around his neck. He was also wearing sunglasses.

"Just pretend we're not here," Principal Blanco told us.

Josh and Andy glanced at each other. Then they both started dancing and singing again:

"Oh, yeah, we're cool . . ."

"Boys!" Principal Blanco snapped. "I thought I told you to stop that."

"But then you told us to pretend you weren't here," Andy pointed out.

"Well, uh, yes, I suppose I did . . ." Principal Blanco mused. "Just do something else."

Josh and Andy sat down at the table again. Meanwhile, the mysterious sunglass people pointed at me and whispered to each other. The whole cafetorium went quiet as everyone watched. The blond sunglass guy aimed his camera at me and snapped a picture. Then he and the sunglass lady headed out of the cafetorium.

As soon as they were gone, a bunch of kids crowded around Josh, Andy, and me.

"What'd they want?" Amanda Gluck asked eagerly.

"They didn't say," I answered.

"Oh, come on," Alex Silver said. "It's obvious. They're looking for an example of your typical jerky kid. Why else would they take a picture of Jake?"

"That's ridiculous," scoffed Julia Sax. "They already know what kids look like. They wouldn't have to take a picture for that."

"Maybe it was for extras!" Andy guessed hopefully.

"But then why did they put the ad in the newspaper?" Amber asked.

Josh, Andy, and I shared a puzzled look. Whatever the sunglass people wanted was a mystery.

4

When school ended, I met my friends at our lockers. We were just about to head home when Principal Blanco stepped out of the main office and waved to me. "Jake, could you come here for a moment?"

"Uh-oh, busted!" Andy grinned.

"What did you do this time?" Josh asked.

"You got me," I answered. "You guys might as well go ahead. I'll catch up with you later."

I went down the hall toward Principal Blanco. He didn't look angry. Instead he had a funny look on his face, sort of like a frozen smile. He put his hand on my shoulder and guided me into his office.

The sunglass people were inside. Only now they weren't wearing sunglasses.

The blond man with the Hawaiian shirt shook my hand. "Jake, my name is Drew DeMille, and this is my associate, Rita Picky," he said. "I assume you've heard that we're from Hollywood."

11

I nodded.

"Good," said Drew. "Have a seat, Jake, we'd like to talk to you."

I sat down. I couldn't imagine what they wanted with me. I didn't know anything about acting. I'd never even acted in a school play.

"Jake," Drew said, "as you know we're here in Jeffersonville to make a new film."

"*Screech Four*?" I guessed.

"Not exactly," said Drew. "But something similar."

"It's about teenagers like yourself," added Rita Picky.

"The point is, we at Priceless Productions try to be as up-to-date as possible," said Drew. "And that means doing our homework."

"Good!" Principal Blanco suddenly interjected. "Homework!"

Drew and Rita shot him an icy look. Principal Blanco shrank back. Drew turned to me. "In the movie business, homework sometimes means having an actor shadow a real person."

"Shadow?" I repeated uncertainly.

"Act like their shadow," Rita explained. "Follow them around for a few days. To get a sense of what their lives are really like."

"Follow them where?" I asked.

"Everywhere," Drew said.

"At home, too?" I asked.

"At home, too," said Drew.

For a moment no one said anything. I guess they were letting the idea sink in.

"Would you mind being shadowed, Jake?" Drew asked.

"Me?" I said, amazed. It was hard to imagine why a movie star would want to shadow me. "Well, uh, I don't know. I guess I'll have to ask my parents."

"Yes," Rita Picky agreed. "We assumed you would. How about tonight?"

5

Both of my parents worked long hours, so my sister Jessica and I didn't have dinner with them until late that night.

"I really wish you kids wouldn't make such a mess of the house," Mom complained as we sat down. "It's not fair that I have to work all day and then come home and straighten up."

"Did you hear about the movie they're making here in Jeffersonville?" Jessica asked, obviously trying to change the subject.

"Why here?" asked Dad.

"No one knows," Jessica said. "But it's the company that does the *Screech* movies. The ones that star Erie Lake."

"Oh, yes." Mom smiled. "The really cute one."

"So there'll be all kinds of traffic and trucks blocking up the streets, and they'll be making noise all night," Dad said wearily. "We'll never get any sleep."

"But think of how cool it will be," Jessica gushed. "There'll be movie stars and directors and producers around."

"Forget it," said Dad. "I don't want anything to do with anyone from any movie company."

Just at that moment, the doorbell rang.

"Who could that be at this hour?" Mom wondered, glancing up at the kitchen clock.

"Actually, it's some people from the movie company," I said.

My father smiled. "That's a good one, Jake."

"No, really," I said, getting up. I went to the front door. Drew DeMille and Rita Picky were outside. "Did you talk to your parents?" Rita asked.

"Uh, sort of," I answered.

"And?" Drew asked anxiously.

"Well, er, I think maybe you should meet them." I led them into the kitchen and introduced them to my parents and sister.

"You're *really* from the movie company?" Jessica asked with wide eyes.

"Yes," said Drew. "I'll be directing the movie. Rita represents the talent."

"What can we do for you?" Dad asked.

Drew explained that they wanted one of the actors from the movie to shadow me.

"You want us to let some *stranger* move into

15

our house and live with us?" my father asked with a frown.

Rita Picky leaned forward. "I wouldn't exactly call Erie Lake a stranger."

Jessica's mouth fell open. *"Erie Lake!?"*

"Never heard of him," Dad said. "You expect me to allow this guy to study my son as if he were some kind of laboratory animal?"

Behind my father's back, Jessica clasped her hands together and made all sorts of pleading gestures to Mom.

"I'm sorry." Dad shook his head. "But I'm not going—"

"To refuse your wonderful offer," Mom quickly finished the sentence for him.

"What?" Dad twisted around and gave her an amazed look.

"Darling, out of all the children at school they chose our son," Mom ad-libbed. "It's an honor. It would be terribly rude to say no."

Before Dad could respond, Mom turned to Drew. "How exactly would it work?"

"Erie would stay in your guest room," Drew went on. "He and Jake would go to school together. Hang around after school. Have dinner with the family."

"Dinner with the family," Jessica repeated dreamily.

Dad looked at her like she'd gone nuts.

16

"That settles it," Mom said firmly.

"Settles what?" Dad asked, totally bewildered.

"It sounds like a wonderful educational experience for the children," Mom said to Drew and Rita. "We'll do it."

6

Rita thought Erie Lake would arrive in Jeffersonville on Saturday night and stay with us on Sunday and Monday.

"There's one favor we'd like to ask," Drew said. "As you can probably guess, Erie Lake draws a lot of attention wherever he goes. We'd really appreciate it if you would keep his visit here a secret."

"Absolutely," Mom agreed. "I assure you that no one in this family will say a word to anyone."

"Wonderful," said Rita. "We'll be in touch."

I showed Rita and Drew to the front door. When I got back to the kitchen my parents were gone. Jessica was on the phone, saying, "You won't believe who's moving in with us! Erie Lake!"

"I thought we were supposed to keep it a secret," I said.

My sister hung up the phone. Her face was flushed with excitement. "I'll make my friends promise not to tell anyone. Can you believe it, Jake? Erie Lake!"

"It's not such a big deal," I said.

Jessica gave me an amazed look. "Get real. He's the biggest star there is!"

"I think you mean he *was* the biggest star," I corrected her. "Didn't his last movie bomb?"

"What? That Shakespeare thing?" Jessica wrinkled her nose. "That was stupid. But it doesn't matter. He's still the star of the *Screech* movies. Everybody rents them on video just to see him."

"I don't," I said.

Jessica rolled her eyes. "It's a *girl thing*, silly."

7

The next morning Josh and Andy were waiting for me outside my house.

"What's that smell?" I asked. The air reeked of bad perfume.

"It's Lakewood, my new cologne," Andy said.

"The stuff that actor Erie Lake sells on TV," Josh told me. "I told Andy you're supposed to *dab* it on. Not paint it on with a roller."

"I hate to say this, Andy, but it smells more like *Swampwood* than Lakewood," I kidded him.

"Maybe to you," Andy countered. "But Erie Lake says girls love it."

"You guys want to walk to school or take the bus?" Josh asked.

"We better walk," I said. "It'll give Andy's cologne time to wear off."

"So what happened with Blanco yesterday?" Josh asked as we walked.

"Oh, uh, he wanted my mom to call him about some PTO thing." I hated lying to my friends, but

Drew said I was supposed to keep the shadowing thing a secret.

We had just reached the school gate when a voice yelled, *"There he is!"*

The next thing I knew, a huge crowd of girls was stampeding toward us from the bus circle. My friends and I froze.

"What's going on?" Josh asked.

"It must be my Lakewood cologne!" Andy realized. "See? I was right! Girls *do* love it!"

8

But as the girls got closer, they started yelling, "Jake! Jake!"

Andy turned to me. "You're not wearing Lakewood, too, are you?"

I shook my head. It was obvious that Jessica's friends had not kept the secret.

Amanda Gluck was the first girl to reach us. "Where's Erie?" she cried.

Andy puffed out his chest. "He's not here, babe, but I am."

Amanda made a face. "Who cares about *you*, Andy? I want the *real* Erie Lake!" She turned to me. "Where is he, Jake?"

"Why's she asking you, Jake?" asked Josh.

Before I had a chance to answer, the rest of the girls arrived, waving autograph books and photos of Erie Lake at me.

"Jake, please get Erie to sign this for me!"

"Jake, can I come to your house to meet him?"

"Jake, will you tell him I love him?"

We were surrounded. As the girls in the back pushed in, the ones in front pressed up against us. My friends and I were squeezed so tight, we could hardly move. Amanda Gluck was right in my face.

"Oh, Jake, I'll do anything to meet him!" she cried. *"Anything!"*

"What's going on!?" Josh yelled as we were jostled by the crowd.

"Take evasive action!" shouted Andy.

"There's Erie Lake!" Josh pointed at the bus circle.

Every head in the crowd turned. "Where?"

"He just went in the cafetorium doors."

Like a swarm of bees, the crowd left us and flew toward the cafetorium.

When they were gone, Josh stepped in front of me. "I think there's something you haven't told us, Jake."

I took a deep breath and let it out slowly as I explained what really happened in Principal Blanco's office the previous day.

"Erie Lake is going to live with you for two days?" Andy's jaw dropped. "I can't believe you didn't tell us!"

"It was supposed to be a secret," I tried to explain.

"Some friend," Josh muttered.

"Yeah," Andy agreed angrily. "Jessica told all of *her* friends."

"She wasn't supposed to," I insisted.

23

"So when is he supposed to get here?" Josh asked.

I gave my friends an uncomfortable look.

"You better tell us," Andy threatened. "It's the *least* you can do after keeping secrets from your best friends."

"Okay, okay." I guess I felt guilty. "He's supposed to come on Saturday night."

"Perfect." Josh grinned. "We'll be there."

9

Even though Mom complained that she hated cleaning the house after working all week, she and Jessica spent Saturday scrubbing and vacuuming. They even did weird stuff like wash the windows and the window curtains.

Dad had to work that day. When he got home, he looked around in wonder. "What's going on?"

"We're having company," Mom called back over the loud hum of the vacuum cleaner while she vacuumed the living room carpet.

"We've had company before and you didn't wash the curtains," Dad pointed out.

"But not a famous movie star," Jessica replied as she polished the coffee table.

"I talked to one of the women at work about this Erie Lake character," Dad said. "Do you know how he got to play the hero in those *Screech* movies?"

"Because he's incredibly good-looking and a great actor," Jessica said.

"That's not what I heard," Dad said. "I heard he got the part because he was the only actor willing to let giant cockroaches crawl all over him."

"That's part of being a great actor," Jessica said.

Dingdong! The doorbell rang. Mom stopped vacuuming.

"You think that's him?" she asked.

"I'll go see." I headed for the front door.

"Wait!" Mom and Jessica both cried at the same time, then dashed upstairs to their rooms.

"What's with them?" I asked Dad.

"You don't expect them to greet Erie Lake in clothes they've been cleaning in all day," he said.

I pulled open the front door. Josh and Andy were outside.

"Is he here?" Josh asked, looking inside.

I shook my head. Meanwhile, Dad shouted up to Mom and Jessica. "False alarm!"

Mom and Jessica came out of their rooms. They were both pulling brushes through their hair.

Beep! Beep! We heard a car horn.

"Now what?" Dad looked outside. Suddenly his expression changed. "Holy smokes!"

"What is it?" I asked.

"The longest limousine I've ever seen," Dad answered.

"Oh, my gosh! It's him!" Mom and Jessica disappeared into their rooms again.

26

"Come on, let's check it out!" Josh went out into the dark. Andy and I followed. The limo was parked at the curb. A row of tiny white lights outlined the back door. The driver's door opened, and a man wearing a gray chauffeur's cap and uniform got out. He walked to the back of the limo and opened the passenger door. It was dark inside, but we could see that the interior of the limo was a deep red color.

My friends and I stood on the front walk and waited for Erie Lake to step out.

Nothing happened.

"Are you Jake Sherman?" the chauffeur asked.

"Yes," I said.

"What are you waiting for?" he asked.

"Erie Lake," I answered.

"He's not here," said the chauffeur. "We have to go get him at the airport."

"Then who's the limo for?" I asked.

The chauffeur smiled. "You."

10

"**W**ay cool!" Andy shouted.

"Let's go!" cried Josh. My friends and I jumped in the back of the limo. Inside, it had two phones, a small color TV, and a bar filled with sodas. A thick dark window separated the driver's compartment from us. I pushed a button and the window went down. Now we could see the back of the chauffeur's head. He could see us in his rearview mirror.

"What's your name?" I asked.

"Charlie," he said.

"Are we allowed to use this stuff?" Andy asked.

"Anything you like," Charlie answered.

"*Yahoo!*" In no time we were all drinking sodas and watching TV.

The Jeffersonville Airport had one short runway surrounded by a tall fence. Charlie drove the limo right onto the runway.

"Just like the movies!" Josh gasped.

"If only the kids at school could see us!" said Andy.

In the rearview mirror, I could see Charlie smile. He parked the limo at the end of the runway. Andy reached for the door handle.

"Wait," Charlie said.

"Can't we get out?" Josh asked.

"You can get out," Charlie answered. "But it's my job to open and close the doors for you."

Charlie came around to the back door and opened it for us. My friends and I got out and stood on the dark runway. The sky was filled with stars. All of a sudden we heard a loud roaring whoosh as a small white jet shot overhead, then banked around in a circle and came in for a landing.

"Unreal!" Josh moaned in awe.

The jet taxied right up to the limo. With our mouths hanging open, we watched as a door just behind the cockpit unfolded and turned into steps.

First Rita Picky came out. Next came a woman with short blond hair, then a man with a long black ponytail. They all started down the steps.

"Who are they?" Josh wondered out loud.

"That's Mr. Lake's entourage," Charlie said.

Andy squinted in the dark. "I don't see any dogs."

"Mr. Lake doesn't have dogs," replied Charlie.

"But you said he had an entourage," said Andy.

"What does that have to do with dogs?" asked Charlie.

My friends and I shared a furtive look. Then I said, "We thought maybe an entourage was a dog."

"An entourage is all the people who travel with the star and take care of him," Charlie explained with a chuckle.

Next, a huge man looked out from the doorway of the jet. His head was shaved almost bald. He had a short black beard and was wearing a dark suit. His neck was as thick as a tree trunk, and his shoulders were so broad they barely fit through the jet's doorway.

"Betcha that's his bodyguard!" Josh whispered.

The big man looked around for a moment, then started down the steps. A moment later, Erie Lake appeared in the doorway.

11

Erie Lake looked smaller than he did in his movies. But there was no mistaking his handsome, chiseled face, or the long black hair that fell into his eyes. As he swept the hair out of his eyes with his hand, I remembered that that was his trademark gesture. He was holding something small in his other hand. He paused and gazed around at the Jeffersonville Airport. Then he started down the steps.

Meanwhile, his entourage reached the limo. Rita Picky stopped when she saw Andy and Josh.

"Who are these boys and what are they doing here?" she asked.

Before I could answer, Josh stepped past me and puffed out his chest. "May I ask who *you* are?"

"I'm Rita Picky, Erie Lake's personal manager," Rita replied in a haughty tone. She gestured to the woman with the short blond hair and the man with the long black ponytail. "This is

31

Marge Peck, Erie's personal trainer and script girl. And this is Herb L. Fern, his personal nutritionist and stylist."

"Well, I am Josh Hopka, Jake Sherman's personal manager," Josh replied, then gestured to Andy. "And this is Andy Kent, Jake's personal . . . uh . . ."

"Friendler," Andy said.

"Hello, everyone," a deep, self-assured voice said behind us.

We all turned to find Erie Lake. Now I could see what he was carrying in his hands. It looked like a medium-size seashell.

"Are we ready to go?" Erie asked.

The big bodyguard and Charlie the limo driver had just finished transferring a bunch of suitcases from the jet to the limo's trunk. We all piled into the limo. With everyone jammed in the back, it wasn't nearly so spacious. Erie gazed down at the seashell in his hands and stroked it gently. The limo went over a speed bump and we all bounced a little.

"You know, Erie, you really don't have to do this," Rita Picky said. "It's not like you've never played a teenager before. All we're doing is wasting two valuable days when we could be shooting."

"I want to do it, Rita." Erie's reply was gentle but firm.

Something reddish stuck its head out of the

seashell in Erie's lap. It had two eyes on long stalks and thin things that looked like antennae. Next, a couple of skinny legs and a red claw appeared.

Erie spoke to it in a soothing voice. "It's okay, Frederick, everything's going to be fine."

My friends and I glanced uncertainly at each other. Erie Lake, world-famous actor, had come to Jeffersonville with his pet crab.

12

A little while later the limo pulled up in front of my house. The lights were all on inside. Through a downstairs window I could see Mom rushing around doing some last-minute straightening. Through a window upstairs I could see my sister brushing her hair.

We all got out and started up the front walk.

"Erie!" A girl I'd never seen before jumped out from behind a bush in my front yard and ran toward the star. But before she could get close, Erie's big silent bodyguard gently scooped her up and carried her away.

"Did you see that?" Josh whispered.

"You mean, the way the bodyguard stopped her?" I whispered back.

"No," whispered Josh. "The way Erie Lake didn't even look at her or stop walking. He acted as if that kind of thing happens every day."

"It probably does," whispered Andy.

My mom opened the front door. "Hi, I'm so glad you — "

Rita Picky walked right past her and into the house.

A few moments later we all gathered in the living room. Rita Picky gazed around with a dismal look on her face. It seemed like she was in a really bad mood. Erie Lake stood in a corner, stroking his pet crab. My mom looked really flustered.

"Uh, Ms. Picky," she said, twisting a kitchen towel nervously in her hands. "I thought only Mr. Lake was staying here. I didn't realize there'd be a group. I don't know how I could possibly put you all up."

"Here?" Rita Picky raised a disdainful eyebrow. "I wouldn't *dream* of it."

I heard footsteps on the stairs. Everyone looked as Jessica came slowly down. Her face was made up and her hair was brushed out. She was wearing her favorite sweater. She paused dramatically on the steps.

Erie Lake blinked at her and then turned to my mom. "Could I see my room, Mrs. Sherman?"

"Of course," Mom said. "You must be tired after your trip. It's just upstairs."

Mom headed for the stairs and the rest of us squeezed past Jessica, who was still waiting to make her grand entrance.

It was kind of funny to see all those people

crammed into our little upstairs hall. Mom and Erie went into the guest bedroom and everyone else crowded around the doorway. Inside the guest bedroom was a wooden dresser and a single bed with a frilly white ruffle.

"Erie! Erie!" From out of nowhere, two screaming girls appeared in our upstairs hallway and tried to squirm past us through the doorway.

Before they could get into the guest bedroom, they were scooped up by the silent bodyguard and whisked away.

"How in the world did they get in here?" Mom asked.

"They didn't come up the stairs," said Jessica.

"They must've climbed in the window!" I realized.

Looking really peeved, Rita Picky turned to my father. "Listen, if you people expect Erie Lake to stay in this house, you're going to have to provide better security, understand?"

Then she turned to Erie. "Erie, baby, for the last time, *please*, don't do this. The production schedule has changed. We don't have the *time*."

Erie Lake sat down on the guest bed. "It's fine, Rita."

Everyone backed out of the room. The big silent bodyguard pulled the guest bedroom door closed and stood in the hallway in front of it.

In single file, we went back down the stairs.

Erie Lake's entourage gathered by the front door.

"Is there anything I should make available to Mr. Lake in case he gets up during the night?" Mom asked Rita.

Instead of answering, Rita turned to Herb L. Fern, the man with the long black ponytail. "What do you think?"

"Just a glass for water," Herb answered. I remembered that he was Erie's personal nutritionist.

"What if there's a fire?" asked Marge Peck, Erie's personal trainer.

Rita turned her gaze on my father. "Are the exits clearly marked?"

"There's the front door and the kitchen door," Dad replied.

Rita rolled her eyes as if she couldn't believe it. "All right, we'll be back in the morning." She and the rest of Erie Lake's entourage left.

"Good riddance," Jessica muttered once they were gone.

Dad yawned. "Well, that was interesting. Now I think I'll go to sleep. You coming, hon?" he asked Mom.

"In a moment," Mom answered. "I just want to bake some muffins for breakfast."

"Excuse me for saying this, Mom," I said, "but you never bake muffins for breakfast."

"I never have famous actors staying here, either," Mom replied.

Dad and Jessica went upstairs. Mom went into the kitchen. That left my friends and me by the front door.

"Pretty amazing, huh?" Andy said.

"So, listen, Jake," said Josh. "You're going to talk to Erie about putting us in the movie, right?"

"I am?" I said, caught off guard.

"You have to, Jake," Andy urged me. "This is our big chance to get a limo."

"And a private jet," added Josh.

"And an entourage," said Andy.

Josh shook his head. "I can live without the entourage."

"Yeah, you're right." Andy turned to me. "Forget the entourage."

I yawned. "I'll do my best, guys."

"See you tomorrow." Josh and Andy left.

Feeling tired, I climbed back upstairs. Erie Lake's big silent bodyguard was still standing in the hallway outside the guest bedroom. He was so big I had to inch my way past him in the hallway to get to my own bedroom.

My bedroom was right next to the guest bedroom. Inside I stood quietly and listened. But I didn't hear a sound. I could picture Erie Lake sitting on the bed, gently stroking his crab.

No offense to all the Erie Lake fans in the world, I thought, but what kind of weirdo walked around with a crab named Frederick?

13

When I woke up the next morning, I could hear the sound of dishes clattering down in the kitchen. Out in the hall, Erie's big silent bodyguard was standing outside the guest bedroom door exactly where I'd left him the night before. I squeezed past him and went downstairs. Tasty aromas wafted out of the kitchen so I knew Mom was busy cooking. When I got down there, Josh and Andy were setting the kitchen table.

"What are you guys doing here?" I asked.

"It's okay, hon," said Mom from the stove. "There's plenty of food."

Dingdong! The doorbell rang and I answered it. It was Marge Peck, Erie's personal trainer.

"Is the gym downstairs?" she asked.

"What gym?" I asked.

"Don't you have a private gym?" she asked.

I shook my head.

Marge looked puzzled. "What do you people do for exercise?"

"We play hoops and football and stuff," I answered.

"There's an old exercise bicycle and some weights in the basement," Mom called from the kitchen.

"That'll have to do." Marge shrugged and went upstairs to get Erie.

Dingdong! This time it was Charlie the chauffeur.

"Smells good," he said and headed for the kitchen. He filled a plate with eggs, bacon, and muffins and sat down at the kitchen table to eat. Josh and Andy loaded up their plates and sat down, too.

Jessica came into the kitchen next. She was wearing her best clothes and had fixed up her hair.

"Since when do you go to church?" I whispered since it was Sunday morning and she was all dressed up.

"This isn't for church. This could be my big chance," she whispered.

"Your big chance for what?" I asked in a low voice.

"You know . . . *with Erie.*"

I stared at her in disbelief. Was it possible that my sister actually thought Erie Lake was going to fall in love with her?

40

Dad came into the kitchen next. When he saw the spread Mom had prepared, he grinned, "Wow, we should have movie stars stay over more often!"

My father, Jessica, and I sat down at the kitchen table with Josh, Andy, and Charlie the chauffeur.

A little while later Erie Lake entered the kitchen followed by Marge Peck and the big silent bodyguard. Erie was wearing a T-shirt and shorts and had a white towel wrapped around his neck. His forehead was dotted with sweat. As soon as he entered, a hush fell over the room.

He took a deep sniff and flashed his famous smile. "Smells good!"

Across the kitchen, my mother began to beam. Erie and Marge filled a couple of plates and crowded around the table with the rest of us. The only person who didn't take any food was the big silent bodyguard. He just stood behind Erie with his arms crossed. Jessica started to blush. My friends and I kept glancing at each other and trying not to grin. Who would believe we were eating breakfast with Erie Lake?

"Erie, what are you doing?" Herb the nutritionist rushed into the kitchen with a horrified look on his face. He was carrying a cooler, like the one we took on picnics and to baseball games. He reached across the table and snatched away Erie's plate.

41

"I thought it was part of shadowing," Erie said calmly. "If I'm going to do everything a teenager does, doesn't that include eating like a teenager?"

"You can shadow all you want," Herb replied. "But as long as I'm your nutritionist, you're going to eat like a human being. Now look what I've made for you." He opened the cooler and placed a plastic bowl in front of Erie. "A nice salad of tofu and egg whites on a bed of crispy lettuce."

"That's *breakfast*?" Andy asked.

"For anyone who wants to live past the age of ninety," Herb huffed.

Josh frowned. "Who would want to live past ninety?"

Bang! The front door slammed. Rita Picky stomped into the kitchen. "Would one of you people please tell my why there is a huge crowd of girls outside?"

Andy went to the kitchen window and pulled back the curtain. Our lawn and the street in front of our house were crawling with girls.

"I thought you people promised to keep this a secret." Rita Picky glared angrily at us.

"How can you keep it a secret when that limo's parked in front of the house?" Andy asked.

"Haven't you people ever seen a limo before?" Rita Picky sniffed.

"Maybe at a wedding or something," Josh said. "But not just parked in front of someone's house."

"What kind of place is this?" Rita Picky asked, shaking her head wearily.

My friends and I shared a look. As far as we knew, Jeffersonville was your basic, *normal* kind of place.

14

Because of the crowd outside, Erie Lake decided to go back to the guest bedroom.

"We could probably sneak out the back," I offered as we climbed the stairs back to the second floor with the bodyguard following.

"Thanks, Jake," Erie said. "I think I'll just relax for a while. Maybe we'll do something later, okay?"

"I'll be around," I said. Erie went into the guest bedroom. Once again, his big silent bodyguard stood outside the door.

After breakfast, Erie's entourage decided to leave. To get rid of the crowd outside, they had Herb the nutritionist put on a coat, hat, and sunglasses and tuck his ponytail under his collar. Rita and Marge escorted him out of the house to the limousine. The crowd of girls thought it was Erie under the coat, and they all jammed around, trying to get autographs. But as soon as Herb got into the limo and Charlie drove away, the girls left.

Meanwhile, my friends and I played basketball in my driveway.

"You think Erie will come out now?" Andy asked.

"I hope so," I said.

But Erie Lake never came out of his room.

Not even for dinner.

That evening, I sat in the den watching TV with Jessica and my friends. Upstairs, the big silent bodyguard stood outside Erie's room.

"I don't get it," Andy said. "I thought Erie was supposed to shadow you. Why'd he stay in his room all day?"

"You got me," I answered.

Josh looked at his watch. "I don't know about you, Andy, but I'm tired of waiting. I'm going home."

"Yeah, I'll go with you," Andy said.

I walked my friends to the door.

"Remember, Jake," Josh whispered so my sister wouldn't hear. "If you see Erie tonight, you have to ask him if we can get parts in the movie."

I bit my lip. "Gee, guys, I don't know."

"Just ask," Andy urged me. "It can't hurt."

My friends left and I went back into the den.

"What was all that whispering about?" Jessica asked.

"Nothing," I said.

"Don't give me that," my sister said. "They want parts in the movie, right?"

I nodded.

Jessica shook her head in disgust. "What nerve. Anyway I'm glad they're gone. Now you can go talk to him."

"Talk to Erie Lake?" I said. "About what?"

"I don't know," Jessica said. "He's been in that room all day. He must be bored by now. You could ask if he wants to do something."

"Why me?" I asked. "Why don't *you* talk to him?"

"Because you're the only one he seems to talk to," said Jessica.

So I went upstairs. The big silent bodyguard was standing in front of the guest bedroom door. As far as I knew, he'd neither slept nor eaten since the night before. I didn't even know his name.

"Excuse me," I said.

The big silent bodyguard turned his head slightly and raised an eyebrow.

"Do you have a name?" I asked.

"Pasha," the bodyguard answered with a heavy foreign accent.

"Pasha?" I repeated, surprised. "What kind of name is that?"

The bodyguard squinted at me menacingly. "Is

46

name my mother give me. You got problem with that?"

"Oh, no," I quickly answered. "I think it's a . . . very pretty name."

Pasha the bodyguard smiled. "Thank you."

"So, Pasha, you think it would be okay if I knocked?" I asked, pointing at the guest bedroom door.

"Is okay with me." Pasha stepped aside. I knocked on the door.

"Come in," Erie said without even asking who it was.

I pushed open the door. Inside, Erie was sitting on the bed, reading a book. On the floor beside the bed was the cooler Herb had brought that morning. Frederick the crab was resting on Erie's chest.

"Hi, Jake." Erie closed the book.

"I didn't mean to interrupt," I said. "You can keep reading."

"No, thanks," Erie said. "I've been reading all day."

"What's the book?" I asked.

"*Huck Finn*," Erie said. "Ever read it?"

"We were supposed to read it in school," I said. "But I didn't."

Erie stood up and stretched. "Neither did I. I mean, when I was your age I never wanted to read anything."

When he was my age? Erie didn't look that much older than me.

"I know this is none of my business, but just how old are you?" I asked.

"How old do you think I am?" Erie asked as he stroked his crab.

I shook my head. "I don't have a clue."

"Twenty-five," he said.

Twenty-five? I couldn't believe it!

Erie smiled as if he'd read my mind. "Hard to believe?"

"Oh, no, no." I tried to cover up my surprise. "I mean, yeah, but you don't *look* twenty-five."

"Ah, yes." Erie sighed wearily. "The curse of my fame."

"Why?" I asked, not understanding.

"I wouldn't be famous if I didn't look young enough to play teenage roles in movies," Erie explained. "But because I look so young I can play *only* teenage roles."

"You're tired of being a teenager?" I guessed.

"Can you blame me?" Erie asked. "Most people are teenagers for seven years of their lives. I've been a teenager for the past *thirteen* years."

"Almost twice as long as the rest of us," I said.

"Right. And now that I'm a famous teenage movie star, the movie companies want to keep me that way," Erie explained. "That's why I have to exercise every day and eat tofu, egg whites, and lettuce."

"Why don't you just refuse?" I asked.

"Because it's in my contract," Erie answered. "No tofu, no jet. No egg whites, no bodyguard. No lettuce, no limo. You want to see a *real* horror movie? Just look at my life."

Erie kept stroking the crab's shell. After a while, Frederick poked out his eyestalks and looked around.

"There's something else I don't get," I said. "How come you didn't shadow me today?"

"No offense, Jake," Erie said, "but I just wanted to get some peace and quiet. I wanted to get away from ringing telephones and screaming fans and overbearing managers. Sitting here and reading all day has been great. I just wish it could last longer."

"Why can't it?" I asked.

Erie looked surprised. "Because the day after tomorrow we have to start shooting *The Creature From the Locker Room*."

"That's the name of the movie?" I asked.

Erie's eyebrows rose. "Oops! It's a secret. Don't tell anyone, okay?"

"Sure. But how come you're not excited?" I asked.

"Sorry, Jake. Been there, done that. *Anyone* could play my part, even you. In fact, you'd probably play it better than me just because you'd be excited about it. You'd bring all your youthful energy to the role."

"What about the script and the lines you have to memorize?" I asked.

"That's nothing," Erie said. "You learn them right before your scene. And if you forget them, you just do another take."

Erie stroked Frederick the crab's head. I stood by the door. It was weird. Erie seemed to imply that acting in teenage movies was easy.

He said *anyone* could play his part.

Even me . . .

Maybe eating tofu and cottage cheese wouldn't be so bad for just *a little* while.

Especially if it meant having the chance to be a movie star . . .

"Erie?" I said.

He looked up from his crab. "Yes, Jake?"

I took a deep breath and let it out slowly. "Suppose I told you I knew a way so you didn't have to do the movie?"

15

Erie gave me a suspicious look. "How?"

"You're not going to believe this," I said. "But I have a machine that can make people switch bodies."

Erie grinned. "How old did you say you are, Jake?"

"Thirteen," I said.

"Aren't you a little old for make-believe?"

"This isn't make-believe," I said.

Erie gave me another look.

"Okay, listen," I said. "Just pretend that you and I could switch bodies. You'd still do your movie, but it would be me doing it in your body. Meanwhile, you'd be in my body just chilling out and having fun and eating anything you liked."

Erie brushed his hair out of his eyes and smiled. "Are you kidding? Of course I'd do it. It would be great to be you, Jake. No one asking for

autographs. No one making me eat healthy food."
With a dreamy look on his face, he sighed. "If only
it could really happen."

"Wait right here," I said.

16

"**I**t looks like a Walkman," Erie said when I came back into the guest bedroom with the mini-DITS.

Months before, my science teacher, Mr. Dirksen, had given me the mini-DITS for safekeeping while he went on an expedition to the Amazon jungle. The mini-DITS was a miniature version of the Dirksen Intelligence Transfer System, which was supposed to transfer knowledge from teachers to students. But it had never worked correctly. Instead of transferring knowledge, all it did was make people switch bodies.

I handed Erie one of the mini-DITS headsets.

"Put it on," I said.

Erie gave me a crooked smile. "Hey, come on, Jake, don't you think we've taken this fantasy far enough?"

"If you don't believe it can really happen, why won't you put on the headset?" I dared him.

Erie raised an eyebrow as if accepting the challenge. "All right, I will."

He started to slide the headset on his head, but then hesitated. "Just one thing."

"What?" I asked.

"I don't believe this can work," he said. "In fact, I'm *sure* it won't work. But just in case it does, we have to agree to switch just for the movie, okay? Once the movie is over, you promise we'll switch back, right?"

"Right." I held out my hand and Erie shook it.

"Okay, Jake," he said with a jocular chuckle as he put on the headset. "Work your magic!"

I put on my headset, then pushed the button on the mini-DITS.

Whump!

17

When I opened my eyes, I was sitting on the guest bed.

Erie in my body was getting off the floor.

"I don't believe it!" he gasped as he stared at me in his body.

"I told you," I said with a smile.

Erie looked down at himself in my body. He raised and lowered my arms, shuffled my feet, and turned my head from side to side. I have to admit that even though I'd switched bodies plenty of times before, it still felt really strange to see someone else moving my head and arms and speaking through my lips.

"Should . . . should I call you Jake or Erie?" Erie in my body asked.

"You better get used to calling me Erie or people will start to wonder," I warned him.

Erie in my body pursed his lips. "You're right, Jake. I mean, Erie. We have to be really careful about this. I'm not positive, but I'm probably violating my contract by being in your body."

"Don't worry, you'll get used to it," I said. Just for the heck of it, I brushed his long black hair out of my eyes the way I'd seen him do it.

Erie in my body clapped. "Very good! So you've switched bodies before?"

"Plenty of times," I said. "I've been in my dog's body, my sister's body. Once I was even in the body of the President of the United States."

"How many people know you can do this?" Erie in my body asked.

"Just a few." I felt my, I mean Erie's, stomach rumble. It felt really empty. "Are you always this hungry?"

"I'm afraid so," answered Erie in my body.

"Why don't you eat?" I asked.

"I have to stay thin," he said. "It's — "

"In your contract?" I finished the sentence for him.

"You got it, Jake, er, I mean Erie," he said.

But Erie's stomach continued to churn hungrily. "Listen, er, Jake," I said. "Can't I go down to the kitchen and have some ice cream or a bowl of cereal? There's no way I'm going to be able to sleep tonight if I don't get something to eat."

"I didn't say you can't eat." Erie in my body kneeled down and opened the cooler Herb the nutritionist had brought that morning. Inside were some apples, a bag of carrots, and a plastic container filled with a brownish-orange liquid. "Help yourself."

"What's in the container?" I asked.

"A vitamin shake," answered Erie in my body. "Try it."

I picked up the plastic container. The thick liquid sloshed around inside. I shook it up, then sipped a little.

"Yuck!" I almost spit it out. "It tastes like bitter tomato and orange juice mixed together. It's awful."

Erie in my body smiled. He reached for the guest bedroom door.

"Where are you going?" I asked.

"Now that I'm in your body, I think I'll go downstairs for a snack." Erie in my body opened the door and went out. But when I tried to follow, Pasha held up his arm to stop me.

"What's going on?" I asked.

"Is past your bedtime, Mr. Erie," Pasha said.

"My *bedtime*?" I repeated.

"It's in your contract," Erie in my body said. "They want you well rested during the shoot."

"But what about something to eat?" I asked.

"If you don't like the vitamin shake, you can have the apples and carrots." Erie in my body had a big smile on his face. He waved and continued down the stairs. "See you in the morning, *Erie*."

18

I ate a couple of carrots and an apple and managed to fall asleep.

Tap . . . tap . . . tap . . . The next morning I was awakened by a faint tapping sound on my door.

"Who is it?" I asked with a yawn.

"Jake," came the reply.

Jake? I was Jake. Then I remembered whose body I was in.

"Come in," I said.

Erie in my body pushed open the guest bedroom door. He was dressed in my pajamas.

"What's up?" I asked with another yawn.

"You are," Erie in my body replied.

"Can't I sleep a little longer?" I asked. "School doesn't start for an hour and a half."

Rap! Rap! Before Erie in my body could answer, someone knocked on the door. "Erie, baby, it's time to get those juices flowing."

"It's Marge," Erie in my body whispered. "Time for your morning exercises, *Erie*."

"Can't I get something to eat first?" I whispered back.

Erie in my body shook my head. "No exercising on a full stomach."

"Let me guess," I groaned. "It's in the contract?"

"No, it just feels better," Erie in my body replied.

Rap! Rap! Marge knocked on the door again. "Come on, Erie. No stalling."

"Just a — " Erie in my body began to answer. Then he caught himself and whispered to me, "Tell her you'll be out in a second."

"I'll be right out," I yelled.

"Okay, Erie," Marge called back. "I'll wait."

"Now listen." Erie in my body looked serious. "Last night before this happened, I didn't really believe we could switch bodies. But now that we have, you've got to promise me that you won't do anything that'll break my contract, okay?"

"How will I know if I'm doing something wrong?" I asked.

"Don't worry," Erie in my body assured me. "They'll let you know." He opened a suitcase and pulled out a T-shirt, shorts, and some cross-trainers. "You better get going."

In Erie's body, I slid out of bed and started to put on his workout clothes. "What are you going to do?"

In my body, Erie yawned and stretched. He patted his mouth, then grinned. "I think I'll go back to bed."

19

For the next forty-five minutes, Marge made me ride the old exercise bicycle in the basement, then do sit-ups and leg lifts and push-ups. Pasha stood at the basement door and watched. By the time we were finished, I was sweaty and *starving*! It was hard to believe that anyone could exist feeling that hungry all the time. I was ready to eat an elephant.

"Time for breakfast?" I asked when the exercise session was over.

"Aren't you going to take a shower first?" Marge asked.

Taking a shower could wait. Breakfast couldn't. On the other hand, if I started messing up Erie's routine, someone might suspect that things weren't normal. "Guess I should take a quick shower, huh?"

Marge grinned as if she thought I was making a joke. "Erie, you've never taken a *quick* shower in your life."

Maybe Erie Lake liked to take long showers, but I was about to break the all-time speed record. Upstairs, Erie in my body was just coming out of the bathroom in my bathrobe. His hair was wet and it was obvious he'd just taken a shower. Once again the sight of him in my body caught me by surprise. From the way he looked at me, I think he was a little surprised, too.

"Have a good workout?" he asked.

"I guess," I answered. "How was your shower?"

"Great," Erie in my body answered. I could tell from all the steam escaping from the bathroom that he must have taken a long one.

I went into the bathroom. Pasha stayed outside and guarded the door as usual.

It turned out that I couldn't have taken a long shower even if I'd wanted to. Erie had used up all the hot water! After a fast, cold shower, I quickly dried off Erie's body, wrapped a towel around his waist, and left the bathroom.

I was passing my sister's bedroom when her door swung open. The next thing I knew, Jessica was standing there. Her hair was fixed up and she was wearing makeup and a pink dress and her party shoes.

"Where are *you* going?" I asked, puzzled.

Jessica batted her mascaraed eyelashes. "To school."

"Why are you all dressed up?" I asked.

"Do you like the way I look, Mr. Lake?" she asked flirtatiously.

Oops! For a moment, I'd forgotten whose body I was in. So, my sister wanted to flirt, huh?

"To tell you the truth, I'm really not into makeup," I said. "I think plain is beautiful. And as far as hair is concerned, I love pigtails."

"Pigtails?" Jessica repeated uncertainly.

"And overalls," I added. "With a plain white T-shirt underneath."

Jessica frowned as if she was finding that hard to believe.

"Try it out," I suggested with a wink and started down the hall to my room.

"Uh, Mr. Lake?" Jessica called behind me just as I was pushing open the door.

"Yes?" I stopped and looked back at her.

"Why are you going into my brother's room?"

I pretended to look surprised. "Guess I got the rooms mixed up."

I went into the guest room and quickly dressed. All I could think about was putting some food in my, I mean Erie's, stomach. I stepped back into the upstairs hall just as Erie in my body came out of my room. We stopped and stared at each other.

Erie in my body smelled a little peculiar. I glanced back at Pasha, then pulled Erie in my body into the guest bedroom and closed the door.

63

"What's that smell?" I asked.

"My hypoallergenic herbal deodorant," Erie in my body answered.

"It makes me smell like a girl," I complained.

"It does not," Erie in my body insisted. Then he leaned toward me in his body and sniffed. "What's *that*?"

"Right Guard," I answered.

"It makes me smell like a *teenager*." Erie in my body wrinkled his, I mean my, nose. "Is it hypoallergenic?"

"I don't know," I answered.

In my body, Erie widened my eyes with alarm. "You better wash my armpits right away."

Wash his armpits?

"Forget it," I said. "I'm going down to breakfast."

20

As I headed downstairs, I could smell fabulous aromas wafting out of the kitchen.

Bacon . . .

Scrambled eggs . . .

Hot cinnamon rolls . . .

By the time I got to the kitchen, my, I mean Erie's, mouth had begun to water, and my stomach was crying out for nourishment. The kitchen was crowded. Charlie the chauffeur, Marge the personal trainer, and Herb the nutritionist were already eating. Rita Picky was the only one not eating. She was just sipping a cup of coffee.

To make it easier to feed everyone this morning, Mom had laid out breakfast buffet style. You took a plate and helped yourself.

Or so I thought.

"Erie!" Herb the nutritionist yelped as I piled my plate high with eggs and bacon and toast. "What in the world do you think you're doing?"

"Having breakfast," I answered. I couldn't wait to eat!

"But you can't eat *that*!" Herb said. "You have to eat *this*." He pointed at a plate with a little mound of white cottage cheese resting on a small bed of green lettuce.

Rita Picky lifted the plate of eggs and bacon out of my hands. "Nice try, Erie baby, but unless you want to go back to Tidal Wave Toilet Cleanser commercials, I wouldn't do it."

I was just about to grab the plate back when I remembered the promise I'd made to Erie about not doing anything that would break his contract.

I slumped down in a chair at the breakfast table and stared miserably at the cottage cheese and lettuce. Just then, Jessica pranced into the kitchen and struck a pose. Her face was scrubbed clean and her hair was pulled into two pigtails hanging down over her ears. She was wearing an old pair of denim overalls and a plain white T-shirt.

While everyone else stared at her, I winked. Jessica broke into a big smile. She put a small helping of eggs and a piece of toast on her plate and sat down.

The next person to enter the kitchen was Erie in my body. When he saw Mom's breakfast buffet, he rubbed his hands together eagerly. "Oh, boy, I have been waiting *years* for this."

Erie in my body piled his plate with eggs, bacon, and hot rolls. Then he sat down at the table. The rest of us watched silently as he cleaned everything off his plate and then got up for seconds. He sat again and started to wolf down his food.

"Ahem!" Jessica cleared her throat loudly.

Erie in my body looked up and realized that everyone was watching him. He scowled for a second, then turned to my mother. "Hey, Mrs. Sher — uh, er, I mean, Mom, this is a great breakfast!"

Mom beamed proudly.

"What's with you, Jake?" Jessica asked. "Why are you acting like you've never seen food before?"

Not realizing that she was speaking to him, Erie in my body kept on shoving food into his mouth.

"Uh, Jake?" I said in Erie's body. "Jessica was speaking to you."

Erie in my body looked up. My, I mean his, cheeks bulged with food.

"Why are you making such a pig of yourself in front of our guests?" my sister asked.

The lines in Erie's brow deepened. "Why are you dressed like a farmer?"

Around the table, people grinned, but Jessica stuck out her chin defiantly. "It just so happens that Mr. Lake told me he really likes this look."

"I have news for you, hon," Rita Picky said.

"Erie likes his women big, blond, and glamorous." She turned to me in Erie's body. "Am I right, Erie, baby?"

Jessica stared at me in Erie's body with a fearful expression on her face. I realized that if I agreed with Rita, I could make my sister look like a jerk. Not that she didn't deserve it, but it would be wrong for Erie Lake to do that.

So instead I just said, "Maybe I've changed."

A look of relief crossed my sister's face. But Rita studied me in Erie's body as if she didn't understand.

"Oh, dear," Mom suddenly said. "It's time for school, everyone."

"There's another big crowd of girls outside this morning," Charlie said.

Rita turned to me in Erie's body. "We'll run the decoy plan. I've got a rental car parked on the street behind the house."

"What decoy plan?" I asked.

The lines in Rita's forehead bunched up. "The one we always use. Charlie will pull the limo into the driveway, and we'll have Jake go out covered by a raincoat. The kids will all think it's you. In the meantime, we'll sneak out the back, go across the neighbor's yard, and take the rental car to school."

What a bummer! Here I was in a famous movie star's body, and not only did I have to eat cottage cheese, but I wasn't going to get to use the limo!

"Here's an idea that will really fool everybody," suggested Erie in my body. "Let's disguise Jessica and put her in the limo and send her over to the high school."

"That's a great idea" Rita said. "Then everyone will think you're at the high school!"

Erie in my body turned to my sister. "And you'll get to ride in the limo."

Jessica looked at Erie in my body in disbelief. "Are you feeling okay, Jake? You're giving up a ride in the limo and giving it to me instead?"

"Hey," Erie in my body leaned over and kissed my sister on the cheek. "Isn't that what little brothers are for?"

Jessica stared at Erie in my body in disbelief. "This is very weird."

21

So my sister got to ride in the limo. Meanwhile, Erie in my body and I in his snuck through backyards with Rita and Pasha and squeezed into a compact rental car.

Rita drove. As we approached Burp It Up Middle School, we saw another big crowd milling around in front. And it wasn't only kids. It was older teenagers and even women my mother's age.

No one paid attention to the compact car in the bus circle. Erie in my body and I in his walked quietly into school. The bell hadn't rung yet, and only a couple of kids were in the halls. They noticed us but just stared and whispered. With Pasha walking ahead of us, no one dared come too close.

We got into homeroom. Ms. Rogers, my favorite teacher, got up from her desk and came over to me in Erie's body. We shook hands.

"Mr. Lake, I'm delighted that you'll be joining

us today," she said with her face turning red. "I have a confession to make. You're my favorite movie star. I've seen everything you've ever been in. Even back in the days when you were Karl in *The Young and the Useless*."

I brushed Erie's hair out of his eyes and flashed his famous smile. "That's very kind of you."

"Now, I assume you'll want to sit with Jake," Ms. Rogers said, "but I'm not sure we have a desk that will fit your, er, friend." She gestured at Pasha.

"He'll stand at the door," Erie in my body said.

Ms. Rogers seemed puzzled that Jake had answered instead of Erie. "If you say so, Jake. Now, I suggest the two of you sit down. That way you'll attract less attention when school begins."

22

The bell rang and we heard what sounded like a stampede coming down the hall. That was weird. I'd been to school early before. Usually the *last* thing kids wanted to do was come in.

As if she knew what was coming, Ms. Rogers positioned herself at the classroom door beside Pasha.

"There he is!" someone screamed. Kids began to crowd into the doorway. Like a policeman, Ms. Rogers held out her arms and stopped them. The only kids allowed in were those who actually had homeroom. Meanwhile the others kept screaming and pushing and holding out pieces of paper and photos for autographs.

Ms. Rogers let Amanda Gluck and Alex Silver in. They both stared at me in Erie's body. I was starting to understand what being a star felt like. It was like being some new exotic animal at the zoo. Josh and Andy managed to work their way through the crowd and into the room. They sat down next to Erie in my body and me in his.

"So, how's it going, Jake?" Josh asked Erie in my body.

"So far so good," Erie in my body answered.

"Andy and I were wondering if you guys wanted to play some B-ball this afternoon," Josh said.

"Sounds like fun," said Erie in my body.

"What about you, Mr. Lake?" Josh asked me in Erie's body.

"I'm up for it," I answered.

"Cool," said Josh.

Meanwhile, Andy quietly slid a fan magazine onto the desk in front of me in Erie's body. On the cover was a color photo of Erie's face.

"My mom was wondering if you'd sign this for her, Mr. Lake," Andy whispered, handing me a black felt-tipped marker.

I took the marker and started to sign. Unfortunately, I'd already written "Ja" before I realized what I was doing.

"Ja?" Andy frowned.

Josh looked over at the magazine. "Ja?"

I glanced at Erie in my body. But with Josh and Andy sitting right there, he couldn't say anything.

Suddenly I had an idea and wrote *Jacob Lakowsky*.

"Who's Jacob Lakowsky?" Andy asked.

"That's my real name," I lied, glancing out of

the corner of my eye at Erie in my body and winking.

"Well, uh, yeah, I guess you probably weren't born with a name like Erie Lake," Andy said, "but for my mom's sake, do you think you could sign it the other way?"

"Sure." Under Jacob Lakowsky, I signed *Erie Lake.*

By now the rest of the class was seated. Just about everyone was staring at me in Erie's body. I didn't know whether to smile back or ignore them. And for some reason Erie's armpits had started to itch, but I didn't want everyone to see me in Erie's body scratch them.

"Ladies and gentlemen, if I could have your attention." Principal Blanco's voice blared out of the speaker on the wall in the front of the room. "As you've probably heard, we have a special guest at Burt Ipchupt Middle School today. His name is Erie Lake, and he is a well-known movie actor. He is here to see what life in middle school is like. Tomorrow his film company will start to shoot a movie in the gym. Therefore gym classes will be canceled for the rest of the week."

"Ya-hoo!" Loud cheering and clapping erupted all over the school.

When it died down, Principal Blanco continued his announcement. "I understand that this must be very exciting for you, but please remember that Mr. Lake is here for business reasons. I expect you to show him every common courtesy and allow him to do the work he needs to do."

Throughout the announcement, everyone stared at me in Erie's body. Meanwhile, the itching in my armpits was getting worse. I started to squirm and move my shoulders around, but Erie in my body noticed and gave me a look, so I stopped.

"Class," Ms. Rogers said from the front of the room. "It's not polite to stare."

Most of the class turned away, except for Amanda Gluck. Meanwhile, Erie's itchy armpits were driving me crazy! I crossed my arms and slid my hands into the pits and started to scratch. Amanda was still looking at me, so I stuck my tongue out at her. She quickly turned away.

The bell for first period rang, but most of us didn't leave our seats because we had social studies next and Ms. Rogers was also our social studies teacher. But there were four minutes until social studies began, and suddenly a small group of kids formed around me in Erie's body.

Alex Silver slid a piece of paper on my desk. I guess he felt that it wouldn't be cool to admit it was for himself, so he said, "Do you think you could sign this, Mr. Lake? It's for my little sister."

"You don't have a little sister," I said.

Alex gave me in Erie's body a shocked look. "How did you know that, Mr. Lake?"

23

"Uh . . ." I felt my, I mean Erie's, mouth fall open. How was I going to get out of this one? Luckily, Julia Sax came to my rescue.

"Oh, come on, Alex," she said. "Admit it. He's right. That autograph's for you."

"Yeah, but — " Alex started to say.

"Don't hog him, Alex," snarled Barry Dunn. "The rest of us want autographs, too."

I signed Erie's name on Alex's piece of paper and then on a bunch of others. Then Amanda Gluck bent down so that her head almost touched the desk. "Would you sign my forehead?"

"Are you serious?" I asked.

"Please?" she begged.

I glanced over at Erie in my body, who didn't look surprised. So I signed his name on Amanda's forehead.

"Oh, thank you, thank you!" Amanda gushed when I was finished. "I swear, I'll never wash my forehead again!"

"So what else is new, Amanda?" Josh asked with a smile.

Everyone laughed. Then the bell rang and Ms. Rogers started social studies.

"Today we're going to begin a new unit on World War One," she announced. "World War One was a war fought in the trenches. Does anyone know what that means?"

At first, no one raised their hands. I couldn't have raised Erie's hand even if I wanted to, because I was too busy trying to scratch his armpits without being noticed. Then Erie in my body raised his.

"Yes, Jake?" Ms. Rogers called on him.

"The soldiers on both sides dug trenches to protect themselves from enemy bullets," Erie in my body answered.

"Precisely," Ms. Rogers said. "Also, until World War One, all wars had been fought either on land or at sea or both. What was different about World War One?"

Once again, no one raised their hands. Erie in my body looked around as if he was hoping someone else would answer. When no one did, he raised his hand again.

"Yes, Jake?" Ms. Rogers said.

"They also fought in the air with airplanes," said Erie in my body.

"Very good, Jake," Ms. Rogers said with a smile. "World War One was fought mostly in Europe, far from our country. Who knows what incident occurred at sea that led to America entering the war?"

Once again no one raised their hands. But this time everyone stared at Erie in my body, as if expecting me to have the answer.

"Everyone seems to think that you'll know the answer, Jake," Ms. Rogers said. "Do you know?"

Erie in my body nodded sheepishly, as if he was embarrassed. "A German submarine sank the British ship *Lusitania*. But the *Lusitania* wasn't a battleship. It was just an ocean liner carrying innocent civilians."

"Once again, you're exactly right, Jake," Ms. Rogers said.

"Show-off," Josh grumbled under his breath.

"And can you tell us why people in our country were so outraged by the sinking of the *Lusitania*?" Ms. Rogers asked.

"Because some of the passengers on the *Lusitania* were Americans," Erie in my body answered.

Ms. Rogers raised an eyebrow. "I'm very impressed, Jake."

Meanwhile, all over the room kids were staring at Erie in my body. Then the wall phone rang and Ms. Rogers went to answer it.

Josh leaned toward Erie in my body and whispered, "What are you trying to do, Jake? Impress Mr. Lake?"

Andy leaned toward me in Erie's body. "Don't be too impressed, Mr. Lake. Jake's usually as big a dummy as the rest of us."

Ms. Rogers got off the phone and continued with class. As soon as everyone turned around, I quickly scribbed a note: *Cut it out! You're making me look bad!*

I passed it to Erie in my body. He frowned, wrote something on it, and passed it back: *I thought I was making you look good.*

Erie clearly didn't remember anything about eighth grade. I wrote back: *That's just it. By making me look good, you're making me look bad!*

Class ended and we left the room. The hall was filled with kids. As Erie in my body and I in his walked behind Pasha, most of the kids stared at me with awestruck expressions on their faces.

"So how *did* you know all that stuff about World War One?" I whispered to Erie in my body as we walked and I scratched my armpits.

"From *Teen Ace*, my third feature film," Erie in my body whispered back. "And for Pete's sake, stop scratching!"

We went into science class. Mr. Dirksen was still away in the Amazon, so we had a permanent substitute named Mr. Grout. Mr. Grout was sort of pudgy and had stiff light-brown hair and beady eyes.

"All right, everyone," he announced as soon as we'd sat down. "Time for a pop quiz."

Mr. Grout was a real sadist. He was always giving us surprise quizzes and extra homework. While the class groaned and moaned, Mr. Grout handed out the sheets. Since I was in Erie's body, I didn't get one. But Erie in my body did. It was all fill in the blanks covering a unit we'd just done on astronomy.

Sitting next to Erie in my body, I watched as he stared down at the test. The first question was incredibly easy: *There are _____ planets in the solar system.*

When Erie in my body wrote *20*, I nearly fell out of my chair! How could he not know that the answer was *9*?

Meanwhile, Erie in my body moved his pencil down to the next question: *The sun's _____ keeps the planets in their orbits.*

Erie wrote *rays*.

This was too much! I glanced at Mr. Grout. His back was turned. With an elbow, I nudged Erie in my body. "It's not rays," I whispered. "It's gravity. And there are nine planets, not *twenty*!"

Erie in my body erased the wrong answers and wrote in the right ones. Then he moved on to the next question. *The most distant planet is _____.*

Erie in my body scratched his head. He didn't know the answer.

"Pluto," I whispered.

Erie in my body gave me a look. "That's not a planet, it's a dog."

"It's also a planet!" I hissed.

"Is there a problem, Jake?" Mr. Grout suddenly asked. Erie in my body and I in his looked up. Mr. Grout was looking right at us.

"Uh, no, sir." Erie in my body and I in his answered at exactly the same moment.

Mr. Grout gave us a suspicious look. For the rest of the test, he kept an eye on us. So there was nothing I could do except watch helplessly while Erie in my body answered all the remaining questions wrong!

24

Out in the hall, we started to walk to my next class. With Pasha leading the way, we were followed by a silent crowd of kids. Luckily for me, Erie's armpits had stopped itching so much. Unluckily for me, his stomach was so empty it felt like it was going to cramp! I can't say it left me in a good mood.

"How could you *not* know that there are nine planets in the solar system?" I asked Erie in my body.

"I've never done a sci-fi movie," he whispered back.

"What are you talking about?" I asked.

"How else would you expect me to know anything about science?" Erie in my body asked.

"Didn't you study it in school?" I asked.

"Who had time to go to school?" Erie in my body whispered. "I've been acting all my life. I've spent most of my life on location."

"You never had any schooling?" I asked, amazed.

"I had tutors," Erie in my body replied.

"So there you go," I said.

"They were *Hollywood* tutors," Erie in my body said. "They taught me to play Chinese checkers. And gin rummy. And solitaire . . . And how to cry on demand."

The next thing I knew, right there in the middle of the hall, Erie in my body started to blink.

"What are you doing?" I asked in his body.

Erie in my body didn't answer. The crowd of kids around us stopped to watch. Erie in my body kept blinking. He made my face look really sad. I watched in disbelief as he made my eyes fill with tears. A moment later, the tears were rolling down my cheeks.

All around us, kids watched in silent shock. Then Amber Sweeny worked her way to the front of the crowd.

"Is something wrong, Jake?" she asked Erie in my body.

"Uh, nothing!" I quickly blurted.

"Then why is Jake crying, Mr. Lake?" Amber asked.

"He's not," I insisted. "I mean, not really."

Meanwhile Erie in my body sniffed and rubbed the tears out of his eyes.

"Cut it out!" I mumbled under my breath. "You're embarrassing me."

"That's not very nice," commented Julia Sax.

"Can't you see he's faking?" I asked.

The silent crowd shook their heads. Amber handed Erie in my body some tissues.

"Thanks," Erie in my body said with a sniff. He dabbed the tissues against his eyes and then blew his nose. Then he crumpled up the tissues in his hand and looked around for a garbage can.

"Could I have them?" Amanda Gluck pushed her way through the crowd, grabbed the used tissues, and jammed them into her pocket. She still had *Erie Lake* written on her forehead in thick black marker.

"Do you think we could get to the next class?" I asked impatiently.

"Gee, what a jerk," someone in the small crowd murmured.

"Hey, it's not his fault," Erie in my body told them.

"That's nice of you to say, Jake," replied Julia Sax. "But just because Mr. Lake's famous doesn't mean he can't be sensitive to other people's feelings."

"I know," said Erie in my body. "But Mr. Lake has a lot on his mind and he's under a lot of pressure. Tomorrow, when his movie starts filming, everything is going to depend on him. Let me show you." Erie in my body turned to Pasha. "If this movie bombs, what will happen?"

Pasha slowly shook his massive head. "Very

bad. Many peoples depend on Mr. Erie. If movie is flop, peoples lose job."

"Gee, I never thought of that," someone said.

Erie in my body turned to the crowd. "A star is only as good as his last movie. Sure, it's cool that Mr. Lake starred in the *Screech* movies. But if his next couple of movies fail, he'll be out on the street faster than last week's stale rolls."

"That *is* a lot of pressure," said Amber Sweeny.

Once again we started down the hall. As we walked, Julia Sax sidled up to Erie in my body.

"I was just wondering, Jake," she said to him in a low voice. "How did you learn so much about show business?"

"Erie and I have been talking a lot," Erie in my body replied, giving me in his body a sly look. "I guess you could say that we've sort of gotten into each other's heads."

25

By lunchtime the story of how Jake Sherman had cried in the hallway was all over school. When girls saw me in Erie's body, they still gave me those dreamy, star-struck looks. But some of the guys pointed at Erie in my body and smirked.

"Why'd you have to cry in the middle of the hallway?" I hissed on the lunch line. "Now you've not only made me *smell* like a girl with that hypoallergenic deodorant stuff, but *act* like one, too."

"Hey, come on, Erie," Erie in my body whispered with a smile. "Can't you have a little fun?"

Maybe Erie in my body was right. But I'd never felt so hungry in my life. And being that hungry made me really crabby. We moved down the lunch line. Pasha walked behind us carrying my tray. They were serving franks and beans for lunch. On the other side of the glass displays, the lunch ladies all stared at me in Erie's body and giggled. A short lunch lady with a big mole on her nose dipped some prongs into a steaming pot of murky hot water and lifted out a dripping hot dog.

"Hot dog, Mr. Lake?" she asked.

Suddenly I saw my opportunity. So Erie wanted to have a little fun, huh?

"Thanks," I said with a big grin. "I'd love one."

Erie in my body immediately leaned over and whispered in my ear, "You know I'm not allowed to eat hot dogs!"

Ignoring him, I turned back to the lunch lady. "On second thought . . . how about five hot dogs?" I gestured to Pasha. "I have to feed my giant, too."

"Did you hear that?' another lunch lady twittered. "He wants *five* hot dogs!"

The short lunch lady with the mole on her nose pressed her lips together tightly for a moment. "Er, we're really only supposed to give one per student, Mr. Lake."

"But I am not a student," I replied in a huff. "I am Erie Lake, international heartthrob and fake crybaby par excellence! I demand that you give me more than one hot dog! My giant is hungry!"

"Cut it out!" Erie in my body hissed in my ear.

"Golly, I don't know — " The lunch lady with the mole still seemed uncertain.

I leaned toward her and stared right into her eyes. "May I ask your name, my dear?"

"M-Martha," she stammered.

"Well, M-Martha, my love, I'll make you a deal," I said. "Five hot dogs for a kiss on the cheek."

"Oh, my gosh!" Martha pressed her hands against her cheeks and blushed. "I don't know what to do!"

The other lunch ladies stopped serving lunch and crowded around Martha, twittering. "Oh, go on, do it, Martha. How often do you get to be kissed by a movie star?"

"But he wants five hot dogs," Martha replied in a quavering voice.

"Well, I don't know about you," said a big husky lunch lady with short hair and broad shoulders, "but I'd sure give him five helpings of baked beans for a kiss."

"I'll take it," I said.

The husky lunch lady dumped five big helpings of baked beans on a plate and handed them to Pasha. At the same time she leaned across the display case, closed her eyes, and puckered her lips.

I let her kiss me on Erie's cheek.

"*Oooooooh!*" The husky lunch lady squealed with delight. "Wait till I tell my husband I kissed Erie Lake!"

That was all it took. Now all the other lunch ladies had to kiss me in Erie's body, too. A few moments later I came out of the lunch line. Pasha walked behind me carrying a tray piled with a mountain of food. Erie Lake's cheeks were covered with red lipstick smudges.

"I can't believe you did that," Erie in my body grumbled as he walked beside me carrying a tray with a container of skim milk, a salad, and Jell-O dessert. "Maybe you've forgotten that I was in *Teenage Ninja Kick-Boxer*?"

"Oh, yeah?" I teased him. "And what did you play? The punching bag?"

Erie in my body and I in his sat down. Josh and Andy came by and joined us. Erie in my body slid the tray with the salad, skim milk, and Jell-O in front of me in his body. Pasha sat down next to me with the tray loaded with huge portions of everything.

"Is okay to eat?" he asked me in Erie's body.

"Go right ahead," I replied.

Pasha picked up a hot dog and finished it in one bite.

Josh was eating *his* hot dog.

Andy was eating *his* hot dog.

Pasha ate a *second* hot dog.

Meanwhile, I was *starving*!

The smell of hot dogs and baked beans was *fabulous*!

In Erie's body, I stared woefully at the salad in front of me. As if they had minds of their own, my eyes traveled over to the tray of food in front of Pasha.

Pasha finished his third hot dog.

There were only two left!

Erie in my body was watching me. "You can't eat any of that," he tried to whisper without my friends hearing.

"You better chill, Jake," Josh warned Erie in my body. "If Mr. Lake wants to eat that, who are you to stop him?"

He was right! Besides, I was *beyond* starving. I was *desperate*. It couldn't hurt to have just a little food, could it?

Pasha picked up another hot dog.

Now only one remained . . .

Just one hot dog.

And a few mouthfuls of baked beans . . .

Herb wasn't around. He'd never know. . . .

That was it. Something inside me snapped. I picked up the last hot dog and opened my mouth and —

"Erie, don't!" Racing through the cafeteria toward us was Herb the nutritionist.

I started to shove the hot dog into my, I mean Erie's, mouth.

"Stop him, someone!" Herb shouted.

Erie in my body lunged across the table and grabbed the hot dog.

"Jake, what are you doing?" Andy yelped.

Pasha grabbed Erie in my body and pulled him away.

Now Herb reached the table. He stretched toward me in Erie's body, slid his fingers into my, I mean Erie's, mouth, and scooped out the hot dog!

"Gross!" Josh and Andy cried at the sight of my half-eaten hot dog in Herb's hand.

"Let me go!" Erie in my body yelled at Pasha, who held him in a bear hug.

Out of the corner of my eye, I saw Principal Blanco hurry into the cafetorium. I looked back at the tray. The hot dogs were gone, but the big plate of baked beans was still there.

I was so hungry!

All I wanted was one spoonful. Just one!

"Not the beans, Erie!" Herb shouted.

I picked up the plate.

Herb grabbed the other side of the plate.

The next thing I knew, we were having a tug of war over the plate of baked beans, which suddenly went flying. . . .

And landed on Principal Blanco's head.

26

"**I** can't believe I'm sitting in the principal's office." Erie Lake in my body sat with his chin in his hands and looked peeved.

"Careful," I cautioned him and tilted my head at Herb the nutritionist and Pasha.

The four of us had been sitting in the office since lunch.

Meanwhile, it seemed like half the school had passed the office and stared in at us — one giant, one grown man with a ponytail, one world-famous twenty-five-year-old actor, and one teenager, all in trouble over a food fight.

"Well, Jake," I said to Erie in my body, "you have to admit, you certainly have had a well-rounded day in middle school."

Erie in my body gave me in his body a droll look. "Very funny."

The last bell rang. School was over. Kids started to flood into the hallways. Principal Blanco came out of his office. Instead of his regu-

92

lar suit jacket, he was wearing a gray Burt Ipchupt Middle School sweatshirt.

He stood over us with his arms crossed and a stern expression on his face. "I hope you've all learned your lessons."

We nodded our heads quietly.

"Food fights are no laughing matter," said Principal Blanco.

We nodded again.

"All right," Principal Blanco said. "You can all go. Except I was wondering if Mr. Lake could stay for just a moment more."

Now what? I wondered while Herb, Pasha, and Erie in my body left the office.

When they were gone, Principal Blanco leaned against one of the secretary's desks. "You start filming tomorrow?"

"Yes," I answered in Erie's body.

"I imagine by now you've cast all the major roles," he said.

"Uh, I guess."

"I just wanted to say that if by any chance you need to fill the role of a principal, I could very well be your man," Principal Blanco said.

Here we go again, I thought with a sigh. *Was there anyone in Jeffersonville who didn't want to be in the movie?*

"It's been a while since I've been onstage," Principal Blanco went on, "but back when I was in college I was in *Hair.*"

"*Hair*?" I repeated.

"Sure, you know," Principal Blanco said. "The original hippie musical." Glancing around to make sure no one could hear, he leaned close to me in Erie's body and whispered, "The one where everyone strips down to their underwear on stage."

Wow! I thought, but I said, "That's very interesting."

Principal Blanco slapped me in Erie's body on the back and led me to the door. "Like I said, Mr. Lake, I'm sure you've got all the roles cast. But if anything should change, you'll think of me, right?"

"Right," I said and went out.

27

Outside school I found Erie in my body waiting with Herb, Pasha, Andy, and Josh.

"So, uh, you ready to play some B-ball, Mr. Lake?" Andy asked eagerly.

Erie in my body and I in his exchanged looks. I felt like we'd gotten into a real rivalry. It was mostly friendly, but there was a serious side to it, too. I wondered what kind of game Erie in my body would play. The guy had to be a wuss. Basketball wasn't the kind of thing you could learn just by making a movie about it.

"Sure," I said, flashing Erie's smile. "Let's do it!"

It turned out that I was wrong. Erie Lake in my body was an amazing basketball player. He had a great outside shot, sneaky, fast inside moves, and solid rebounding. No matter how we divided up, the team with Erie in my body usually slaughtered the other team.

"Geez, Jake," Andy said to Erie in my body. "I've *never* seen you play so well."

"Yeah," Josh agreed as he panted. "If I didn't know any better, I'd swear you were a whole different person or something."

His words hung in the air.

He and Andy shared a look, as if they weren't sure. . . .

Then Josh shook his head. "No," he said. "It couldn't be."

"It's almost dark," said Erie in my body. "Let's play one last game."

This time the teams were Josh and me in Erie's body against Andy and Erie in my body.

Thanks to some lucky shots by Josh, the game was soon tied 10 to 10.

"Next basket wins," Andy said, panting for breath.

I really wanted to show Erie that I was a decent ballplayer too.

Josh got the ball.

I cut behind Andy and got free.

Josh passed the ball to me in Erie's body.

I drove toward the basket.

Erie in my body left Josh to cover me.

There was only one way I could make the shot.

It was going to take everything I had.

It was going to take . . . the reverse spinning fadeaway layup!

I made the move and shot the ball.

It hit the backboard and rolled around the rim!

Once!

Twice!

It fell in!

"Ya-hoo!" In Erie's body I jumped up and shouted, then turned to Josh to give him double high fives.

But Josh just stood there with his arms crossed and a funny look on his face. "Nice shot . . . *Jake.*"

An awkward moment passed. Erie in my body, Andy, Josh, and I in Erie's body stood panting for breath and pulling our sweat-soaked shirts away from our bodies to cool off.

Then Erie in my body cleared his throat. "You're mistaken, Josh. I'm Jake."

But Josh and Andy just stared at me in Erie's body with astonished looks on their faces.

I swallowed nervously. "You know, it's probably time to head home."

No sooner were the words out of my mouth than the limo pulled into the school driveway. Erie in my body and I in his shared a look.

"Go ahead, take the limo," said Erie in my body. "It's a nice evening. I think I'll walk."

He started to walk away.

Josh looked at Andy and then at me in Erie's body. I could almost read my friend's mind: *Why would Jake be telling Erie Lake to take the limo?*

Charlie the driver hopped out of the limo and opened the back door for us. Suddenly, Josh stepped toward me in Erie's body and cupped his hand over my ear.

"Tell Pasha to sit in the front," he whispered.

"Why?" I asked.

Instead of answering me, Josh smiled knowingly as if he'd just figured something out.

"What's going on?" I asked in Erie's body.

"Just do it," Josh insisted.

I turned to Pasha and told him to sit in the front with Charlie. Then my friends and I got in the back.

"Boy, I sure am glad this thing has a bar," I said, taking out a can of Coke. "You guys want something to drink?"

Josh didn't answer. Instead he flicked the switch that raised the dark glass partition between us and Charlie and Pasha in the front. Then he turned to Andy. "You still have that magazine he signed this morning?"

"Yup." Andy pulled it out of his backpack.

In the back of the limo Josh flicked on a light and studied the signature.

"Jacob Lakowsky," he said to himself. "Jacob starts with J, A."

"Just like Jake," said Andy.

"What are you guys talking about?" I asked, pretending not to know.

Josh didn't even bother answering. Instead, he started thumbing through the fan magazine. Suddenly he stopped and smiled. Then he looked up at me in Erie's body. "You're busted, dude."

Inside the magazine was a black-and-white photo of Erie with his autograph. Josh flipped back and forth between Erie's real signature and my fake attempt at it.

"How'd you get him to do it, Jake?" Josh asked.

"Do what?" I asked back, still clinging to the hope that I could convince them it wasn't me in Erie's body.

"Cut the bull, Jake," Andy said. "We know it's you inside there."

"I honestly don't know what you're taking about," I insisted.

Andy and Josh shared a look.

"Can you believe this guy?" Josh asked. "He says he's our friend and then he goes and does something like this and doesn't even tell us. I mean, after all the stuff we've been through together."

"Well, you know how Jake is," replied Andy. "He wasn't even going to tell us that Erie Lake was coming to live with him. He just wants all the fun for himself. Forget about him ever sharing."

"You're right," Josh said. "What was I even thinking?"

"Would someone *please* tell me what's going on?" I asked in one last attempt to pretend I was Erie.

"I'll tell you what's going on." Josh leaned forward. "Earlier today you signed Erie Lake's name on a magazine, but it looks nothing like his real signature. Then in basketball you did that reverse spinning fadeaway layup. There's no way Erie Lake could know that shot. And then, a few moments ago I, a measly eighth-grade nobody, told *you*, Mr. Erie Lake, world-famous superstar, to tell Pasha to sit in the front of the limo. And you asked why."

"Okay." That was all true.

"Well, let me tell you something, dimwit," Josh said. "If Erie Lake was in that body, he never would have asked why. He would have told me to get stuffed."

"Josh is right," Andy added. "You blew it, Jake. You may *look* like a star in Erie Lake's body. But you sure don't know how to *act* like a star."

I knew they were right.

"Okay, okay," I finally admitted. "Erie and I switched bodies."

"Why?" Andy asked.

"He said he was really tired of playing teenage roles and that I could probably do a better job just because I'd be more excited about it," I said.

"So you're going to act in the movie?" Josh asked.

"I guess," I said. "Why not?"

Josh start to pout. "This is totally unfair."

"Wait a minute!" Andy cried and pointed at me in Erie's body. "You're the star of this movie!"

"So?" I answered.

"Now you can *definitely* give us parts!" Andy exclaimed.

"That's right!" Josh realized. He turned to Andy and slapped him five. "Andy, my friend, you're a genius."

28

In the back of the limo, Josh and Andy sang for the rest of the trip home.

"Oh, yeah! What a scene! We'll be on the big screen!

We're cool! We're news! You can read our interviews!

We'll be on all the TV shows!

If we look too shiny, please powder our nose!

It must be time to fix my hair!

We'll be on posters everywhere!

Fan mail comes in a big boxcar!

We'll see you when we win next year's Oscar!"

My friends were totally stoked. I had to admit they were right. We'd always been in this body-switching thing together. It wasn't fair for me to hog the spotlight this time and leave them with nothing to do.

Charlie dropped Andy and Josh off at their

houses and then took me in Erie's body and Pasha home. There were no crowds waiting this time. I let myself and Pasha into the house and went upstairs. From all the steam in the bathroom, I figured that Erie in my body had already taken a long shower. The door to my bedroom was closed. No doubt Erie in my body was inside reading Mark Twain books and petting his pet crab, Frederick.

Pasha yawned, then quickly tried to cover his mouth with his hand.

"It's okay, Pasha," I said. "You've been up for days. You must be pretty tired."

"I be okay," Erie's bodyguard insisted.

"There're no kids around," I said. "No one's crawling in any windows. Why don't you go downstairs and stretch out on one of the couches and get some sleep?"

"You are sure, Mr. Erie?" Pasha asked.

"Yes."

Pasha went downstairs, and I went into the bathroom and took another cold shower.

A little while later I let myself out of the bathroom. From downstairs came loud snoring, so I knew Pasha was asleep.

I was passing my sister's bedroom when Jessica opened the door. She was still dressed like a farmer.

"Mr. Lake?" she said.

"Yes?"

"You're going to start filming the movie tomorrow?"

"That's right."

Jessica bit her lip. "So I guess you'll be really busy."

"I guess," I said in Erie's body.

An awkward moment passed. Then my sister stretched forward and kissed me in Erie's body on the cheek. "It's been nice having you here, Mr. Lake."

"No sweat," I said and headed downstairs.

When I got to the bottom of the steps, I looked back up. Jessica was leaning in her doorway with a sad, dreamy look on her face.

Down in the kitchen I called Rita Picky at the hotel where she and the others were staying. She wasn't happy when I told her I wanted Josh and Andy to get roles as extras, but she said she'd arrange it.

29

It was still dark the next morning when I felt a hand shake my shoulder. I opened my eyes and looked up to find Rita Picky. "Wake up, Erie, baby, it's show time."

"Wha?" I yawned.

"We start filming at seven," Rita informed me in Erie's body. "Time to get in your trailer and get ready."

"What time is it?" I asked.

"A little after four," she said.

"In the *morning*?" I couldn't believe it! I rolled over and pulled the pillow over my head. "I want to sleep."

I felt Rita shake my shoulder again. "Erie, don't play games with me. You know how much is riding on this film. It's your career, baby. If this movie doesn't make it, you really will be back to making commercials for Tidal Wave Toilet Cleanser. Now, come on, baby, we're all depending on you."

Rita went to the door and flicked on the light. I had to shield my eyes from the glare. She went out and closed the door behind her. For a moment I just lay there in bed. That's when I remembered what Erie in my body had said in school. They really were all depending on me. Rita, Pasha, Charlie, Herb, Marge. All of their jobs depended on Erie Lake.

I took a shower, then went back into the guest room and put on some clothes. It was weird. Even though I was in a movie star's body and hundreds of kids wanted my autograph and millions of people wanted to see my movies, in a strange way I felt all alone. So much depended on me. All those people who wanted my autograph or wanted to see me — but that was *all* they wanted. They really didn't want to know me. They really didn't want to hear what it was like to feel all this pressure.

When I came out of the guest room Jessica was standing in the doorway of her bedroom, wearing her bathrobe. She leaned forward and kissed me in Erie's body on the cheek. "Break a leg, Mr. Lake."

I went down to the kitchen. Mom was up. Once again she'd made everyone breakfast and coffee. It smelled great, but none of it was for me in Erie's body. Herb had taken care of my breakfast. This morning it was a bowl of nonfat yogurt with wheat germ.

I shook Erie's head. "Sorry, Herb, I don't think I can stomach it this morning."

All around the table people gave me in Erie's body worried looks.

"It's going to be a long day, Erie," Herb said. "You'll never get through it on an empty stomach. How about a vitamin shake?"

"Okay, Herb," I agreed, mostly so that the others would feel better. "One vitamin shake . . . to go."

Herb used the mixer to whip up a shake. He poured it into a plastic container. As we left the kitchen, Mom gave me in Erie's body a kiss on the cheek. "Break a leg, Mr. Lake."

There were no girls waiting outside in the dark at five in the morning. My entourage and I piled into the limo.

"Why does everyone keep telling me to break a leg?" I asked as Charlie pulled the long limo from the curb.

Rita smiled uncomfortably. "You're joking, right, Erie?"

I shook Erie's head.

Rita and the others exchanged a nervous look.

Marge leaned forward. "It's what everybody says, Erie. It's the traditional way of saying good luck in show business."

No one spoke for the rest of the trip.

We got to school. The parking lot next to the gym was filled with trucks and vans and trailers.

The limo pulled up to one of the trailers. Charlie got out and opened the door for me.

"Well?" Rita said.

"Well, what?" I asked.

Rita wrinkled her brow. "This is your trailer, Erie."

"Oh." I started to get out of the limo.

"Erie?" Rita called behind me.

I stopped and looked back to her. "Yeah?"

"Are you okay?" she asked.

"Sure," I said.

I left the limo and climbed into the trailer. Herb followed me. Pasha stayed outside. Inside, the trailer was set up like a dressing room with a makeup table and a big mirror lined with lightbulbs. Farther back were racks of clothes. Herb started to pull some clothes off the rack.

"Okay, Erie, baby, first we'll get you dressed," he said, holding out the clothes toward me in Erie's body.

I took the clothes and went into a changing room. When I came out, Herb was waiting by the makeup table with Marge, Erie's personal trainer. I hesitated when I saw her. Was she going to make me exercise now?

"Come on, Erie, baby." Herb gestured at the makeup table. "There's no time to lose."

I sat down and Herb started to fix my hair and brush makeup on my face. Meanwhile, Marge opened something that looked like a script. Inside, some of the lines were highlighted in yellow.

"Here are your lines, Erie," she said.

So while Herb worked on my hair and makeup, Marge went over the script with me in Erie's body.

"Wait a minute," I said after we'd gone over some of my lines. "This stuff sounds more funny than scary."

Marge gave me in Erie a crooked smile. "Of course it is, silly. It's a spoof of a horror movie. This is your first comedy, remember?"

"Oh," I said. *So that's what the big secret was!*

We kept reviewing my lines. Outside, the sky began to turn gray and more people started to arrive. I saw Andy and Josh. That meant Rita had called and told them they could have small parts in the movie. Then I saw Erie in my body on the set. I had to assume that Rita let him come as a reward for the shadowing.

Someone knocked on the trailer door and called out, "Erie Lake needed on the set."

"Okay, baby, you're on," Marge said. "Break a leg."

This was it. I was about to act in my first movie.

30

I got up and left the trailer. Outside, a guy carrying a walkie-talkie started to lead me in Erie's body into the school gym. We passed electricians carrying lights and carpenters hammering props. A generator truck rumbled, and half a dozen heavy black electric cables snaked into the gym through a window. It was weird. Here on the set, hardly anyone paid any attention at all to me in Erie's body.

We went through the gym and into the boys' locker room. Inside, a big crowd of people was bustling about. Some were setting up cameras. Sound people were adjusting mikes. Lighting people were aiming lights. The guy with the walkie-talkie led me in Erie's body through the crowd. Ahead of us, Drew DeMille, with the blond hair and Hawaiian shirt, was sitting in a director's chair. He held out his hand.

"Good to see you this morning, Erie," he said. "Ready to go?"

"Sure thing," I said.

"Great." Drew clapped his hands together and turned to the crowd of technicians. "Okay, people, let's do it!"

The next thing I knew, I was standing at a gym locker. The bright lights were shining on me in Erie's body. They felt really hot. The camera was aimed at me. A big boom mike hung over me. Through the crowd came a weight lifter with the most muscular arms I'd ever seen. His right arm was covered with green slime makeup and red fake blood.

"Okay, Erie," Drew said from the director's chair. "You're a typical student coming into the locker room to change into your gym clothes. You do the combination and open your locker. The monster's arm bursts out and grabs you around the neck. You struggle to fight it off. Make it a good, long struggle. Put a lot of energy into it."

"Got it," I said.

The big muscle guy with the monster arm went around into the aisle behind my locker.

"Okay, everyone, quiet on the set," Drew yelled.

Everyone got quiet. There must have been twenty-five people watching me in Erie's body.

"Sound," Drew yelled.

"We've got sound," the sound man called back.

"And . . . action!" Drew yelled.

I started down the aisle, stopped in front of the

111

locker, and opened it. Instantly, the monster arm lunged out and grabbed me in Erie's body by the neck. I pretended to struggle before finally breaking free.

"Cut!" Drew called. Behind him the crowd politely clapped.

"That was good, Erie," said Drew. The big muscle guy came out from behind the locker. "This time, let's try it with some suspense. Erie, you open the locker and look in the mirror you've got hanging inside. Three or four seconds pass while you check your hair, and *then* the big arm comes out and grabs you. Got that?"

The big muscle guy and I both got back into our positions. Drew yelled, "Action," and we did the scene. When we finished, the crowd clapped again. I sensed that they thought the scene was okay but not great. Meanwhile, Drew looked over at Rita Picky, who was busy speaking into a walkie-talkie.

"What do you think?" he asked.

Rita looked up. "It needs something more."

Drew rubbed his chin pensively. I got the feeling he wasn't sure what to do.

"You know what could be funny?" I asked.

Drew looked up, surprised. "What, Erie?"

"A lot of guys just dump their gym clothes in the bottoms of their lockers," I said. "What if I open the locker, and just as the monster's arm is about to get me, I kneel down to get my stuff. So the arm misses, then swings around grabbing for me. Meanwhile, I'm under it getting my gym clothes, and I don't even know it's there. Maybe I even slam the locker door on it by accident."

Drew looked stunned. "That's . . . that's a *great* idea, Erie."

Rita Picky put down her walkie-talkie and looked amazed. "Erie, baby, that's fabulous!"

After that, we did about ten more takes, each time trying something different that I suggested.

"That's a wrap!" Drew yelled one last time. He had a big grin on his face. Behind him, the crowd of onlookers clapped really hard. Someone even whistled. You could see that they thought we'd done a good job.

31

"That was great, Erie!" Drew patted me hard on the back while the technicians packed up the lights and started to move the camera.

"What do I do now?" I asked.

I didn't know why, but everyone laughed.

"You can go back to your trailer and rest, Erie," Drew said. "Take it easy and prep for your next scene. We'll let you know when we need you again."

I have to admit that I was pretty bushed. As I started to weave through the crowd, people patted me on the shoulder.

"Way to go, Erie."

"Good work."

I got through the crowd and found Rita walking beside me. "Erie, baby, that was incredible! I haven't seen you that focused on your work since *Screech One*. And even then you never made suggestions like you did today."

I had to smile. "Must be a whole new me."

We stopped outside Erie's trailer. "All I can say is, keep it up, Erie," Rita said.

I climbed into my trailer. Inside, Herb gestured to the makeup table. He had a big smile on his face. "Erie, baby, the buzz is hot. Way to go!"

I sat down. Marge came in. "Oh, Erie, everyone's talking about how great you were!"

We did four more scenes that day. Each time we started with the script, but after that we'd make up other ways to do it. Andy and Josh got to be extras in two of the scenes. Everyone seemed incredibly excited and kept talking about how I was acting like a new Erie.

At the end of the day, I was back in the trailer trying to catch my breath while Herb took the makeup off my face. A stream of people came in to congratulate me in Erie on how hard and well I'd acted that day. First came Drew, then a bunch of people in fancy clothes who I didn't even know. Everyone kept talking about the incredible buzz and excitement on the set.

By the time they all left, it was dark.

"Ready to go home, Erie?" Herb asked.

"In a second," I said. "You go ahead. I just want to be alone for a moment."

"I don't blame you," Herb said.

He left the trailer. For the first time all day I could finally relax. Wow, what a day! So this was a movie star's life. It wasn't easy, but when things were going well, it was pretty cool.

Someone knocked on the trailer door. "Come in," I called.

The door opened and Erie Lake in my body stepped into the trailer.

32

"**N**ice going," he said. "Everyone says you were fantastic."

"Uh, thanks," I said.

"So, uh, what's next?" Erie in my body asked. I could tell there was something on his mind.

"I guess I go home and rest up for tomorrow," I said.

Erie in my body fidgeted a little, then shoved his hands in his pockets.

"Something wrong?" I asked.

"I have a confession to make," he said. "I lied when I told you I was bored with acting and tired of being a movie star."

"Then why —" I began.

"I was scared," said Erie in my body.

"Of what?" I asked in his body.

"Doing a comedy," he said. "I've never done one before, but after watching you today, I see that I can do it. So I want to switch back to my body."

"Now?" I asked.

"Yes, now," said Erie in my body.

I didn't know what to say. I didn't want to switch back now. I wanted to keep acting in this movie. I wanted to see what I could do. I liked it when people congratulated me on the job I was doing. I liked it when people treated me like I was famous.

The trailer door opened and Rita Picky stepped in.

"Excuse me, Jake, what are you doing in here?" she asked when she saw Erie in my body.

"I, huh, I was just congratulating Erie on the great job he did today," Erie in my body answered.

"That's very nice of you," Rita said. "But you better get going now. Erie has to rest up for tomorrow."

"Right." As Erie in my body backed toward the trailer door, he turned to me. "You have to do it, Jake." He went out and closed the trailer door behind him.

Rita turned to me with a puzzled look. "Erie, baby, what was that all about? Why did he call you Jake?"

"I, uh, don't know," I quickly answered and stood up. "I'm sure it was nothing. Guess we better go, huh?"

"You bet," Rita agreed. "You must be exhausted. Let's get you back to the hotel so you can rest."

I stopped. "The hotel? Why about my, er, I mean, Jake's house?"

"Why would you want to stay in that dump?" Rita asked. "You've finished shadowing him. Production has begun. We're paying for a beautiful room in the hotel for you. You need to go someplace where you can relax and rest."

"But that's why I need to go to Jake's," I said. "I find it, er, very relaxing. And *inspiring*. I mean, how do you think I got all those ideas today?"

Rita Picky frowned and scratched her ear. "Okay, Erie, if you really feel you need to stay at the Shermans' to do the kind of work you did today, then I'll arrange for you to stay there."

33

It was late when I got home. Rita said she'd pick me up in the morning. Suddenly I felt really hungry. I went into the kitchen hoping there'd be something Erie Lake was allowed to eat.

But I was in for a surprise. When I got into the kitchen, Erie in my body was sitting at the kitchen table with Josh, Andy, and Jessica. My friends and sister glared at me.

I turned to Erie in my body. "You told them?"

Erie in my body pointed at Josh and Andy. "Turns out these two already knew."

"You tricked me into wearing farm clothes," Jessica sniffed.

"Erie says you tricked him, too," said Josh.

"You told him the mini-DITS was just a fancy Walkman," said Andy.

"Just like you did with Ted," added Josh.

"Who?" I asked.

"Our counselor at Camp Grimley, remember?" Andy said.

"That's not true!" I argued.

I could tell from their looks that they didn't believe me.

"I think you better switch back," suggested Josh.

"Why?" I asked.

"Because it's not fair that you get to be a star and the rest of us don't," said Andy.

"But I got you roles in the movie, didn't I?" I asked.

"That's totally beside the point," said Jessica. "Jake, it's not fair for you to take Erie's body. Erie spent years struggling. He risked everything to be a star. And now that he's done all that hard work, you're trying to take the reward away from him."

"No, I'm not," I protested. "We agreed that we'd switch just for this movie. When the movie's over, we'll switch back."

"Will we?" Erie in my body asked. "Or when the movie's over will you say, 'Know what? This is fun. Why don't we just wait until the movie comes out?' And after that it will be some other excuse. You said it yourself, Jake. *Everyone* wants to be a star. It's just that unlike you, most stars had to work really hard to get there."

"I know that," I replied.

"Okay, then," said Josh, "if you're so agreeable to all this, suppose you just agree to switch back with Erie right now?"

"Uh . . ." I didn't know what to say.

"Well?" My sister Jessica drummed her fingers against the kitchen table impatiently.

"We had an agreement," I argued. "We said we'd switch back when the movie was over."

Erie in my body turned to the others. "See? He doesn't want to do it."

"Yes, I do," I insisted. "Just . . . not quite yet."

"I'm really disappointed in you." Jessica poured the guilt on thick.

"I can't believe you'd do this to me," Erie in my body said.

"It's totally unfair," added Josh.

I turned to Andy. He was my last hope. "Do you really agree with them?"

"Well, uh, here's what I think," Andy said. "If you're gonna stay in Erie's body, could I have your skateboard?"

34

I wound up spending that night in the hotel after all. My sister, Erie in my body, and my friends bugged me so much that I had no choice but to go out to the limo and ask Charlie to drive me in Erie's body there.

The next morning Rita and I took the limo back to school. "Just keep up the great work, Erie," she said. "Everyone's talking about how this movie is going to put you back on top where you belong."

In the school parking lot I climbed into the trailer. Herb began to put makeup on me. Then Marge came in with the script.

"Ready for your big shower scene?" she asked brightly.

"Me in the *shower*?" I replied uncertainly.

"Sure, Erie," she said. "You know, you've done a million of them."

"Uh, right." I played along. "And it's always shot from the waist up."

"If it's not, we've got those flesh-colored shorts so no one can tell the difference," she said.

"Right," I said, feeling a lot better.

"The only problem is what to do about the water," Marge said. "The tarantulas hate water."

"Tarantulas?" I swallowed.

"Oh, Erie, you're pulling my leg again," she said with a chuckle. "You know how Drew's been talking for months about this scene. It's going to be the biggest, creepiest bug scene ever. Even bigger than the time you fell into that hot tub filled with giant cockroaches in *Screech One*."

"Me and tarantulas in the shower?" I grimaced. "The biggest bug scene ever?"

"And you better not step on any," Marge warned, "because those critters are not cheap."

I sat there stunned while she described the scene. Erie was going to be alone in the shower when the tarantulas started to pour in from every direction. Then the scene would be stopped and the special-effects people would stick a bunch of fake tarantulas all over my body. But to make the scene look really real, they would heap hundreds of *real* tarantulas over the fake ones. The way Marge described it, Erie would be totally covered by those big, hairy spiders.

The biggest bug scene ever!

At that moment, I glanced out the window and saw Josh walking across the parking lot carrying a day pack. "Uh, could you excuse me for a moment?" I asked.

"Sure, Erie," Marge said. "But make it fast, okay?"

I hurried out to the parking lot. Josh squinted angrily when he saw me in Erie's body.

"I just want to talk to you, okay?" I said.

"What about?" Josh asked.

I looked around. Once again, the parking lot next to the gym was filled with technicians and carpenters. "Let's take a walk," I said, leading him toward the trees on the other side of the parking lot.

"So what's up?" Josh asked.

"I've been thinking about last night, Josh," I said. "And I think maybe you're right. Maybe it is wrong for me to steal this movie away from Erie. But I just wanted to make sure that was how you *really* felt and that you weren't just saying it because Andy and Erie and Jessica were there."

"No, I really meant it," Josh insisted.

"So you honestly think I should give up all this incredibly fantastic glamorous fun and return Erie's body to him?" I asked.

I can't say I was surprised when Josh hesitated a little. "It's really *that* much fun?"

"A total blast, Josh," I said in Erie's body. "You can't even begin to imagine."

Josh tugged thoughtfully at his ear. "I still

think you should give Erie his body back, Jake. But before you do — I was just wondering. I mean, you and I have been friends for a really long time, right, Jake?"

"Right," I answered in Erie's body.

"And we've been through a lot of weird stuff together," Josh said.

"That's true," I agreed.

"And in all that time I really haven't asked very much from you," Josh said.

I gave him a look. "Well, I don't know about *that*."

"*Okay, okay,*" Josh admitted. "Forget I said that. All I mean is that I've been a pretty good friend."

"So what's your point?" I asked, pretending I didn't already know.

Josh glanced to his left and right as if making sure no one was watching. "I really, really think you should give Erie his body back. It's just that . . ."

"Just what?" I asked.

"Do you think you could give it to me for a day first?" he asked hopefully.

"Erie's *body*?" I pretended to be shocked.

"Hey, come on. Aren't good friends supposed to share?" Josh demanded.

"Well, I guess," I said in Erie's body.

"Then what's the problem?" he asked.

"I guess the problem is that I know we share stuff like skateboards and CDs," I said. "I just never thought that included famous bodies."

"Hey," Josh said. "CDs, skateboards, famous bodies, whatever."

"Erie!" It was Marge, waving to me from the trailer. "Come back, we have to get you ready."

Josh gave me in Erie a worried look. "There's not much time."

"You're right," I said. "We'll never have time to get back to my house."

"Why do we have to do that?" Josh asked.

"To get the mini-DITS," I said.

Josh gave me a guilty look, then slid his day pack off. "Actually, I have it right here."

35

"**W**hat are you doing with the mini-DITS?" I asked.

"Well, uh . . ." Josh paused and coughed. "See, after you went to the hotel last night, we came up with this plan."

"Plan?" I repeated.

"Yeah," Josh said. "Erie convinced us that we had to grab you just before lunchtime today and get you into the trailer and switch him back into his body and you into yours. . . . You're not mad, are you?"

"Mad?" I repeated. "Heck, no. I mean, like I said, I understand the way you feel."

"And you're still willing to switch with me instead of Erie?" Josh asked hopefully.

"*Erie! Come on, they need you on the set!*" Marge called.

"Sure, Josh," I said. "You deserve a chance to be Erie, too. But we better do it fast."

"Okay." Josh handed me in Erie one of the

mini-DITS headsets and I slipped it on. He put on the other one.

"Ready?" he asked.

"Ready," I replied in Erie's body.

Josh pushed the button.

Whump!

36

When I opened my eyes, I was staring at Erie Lake. Only now Josh was in his body.

"Cool!" Josh looked down at his new body. Then he looked at me in his body. "Thanks, Josh. Oops! I'm Josh. I mean, thanks, Jake, I really appreciate this."

"*Erie?*" Marge called again. "*You must come now!*"

"Guess I better go," said Josh in Erie's body.

"Just remember to run your fingers back through your hair and flash that famous smile," I said. "That's Erie's trademark."

"What about the movie?" Josh in Erie asked.

"Just do whatever they tell you and you'll be fine," I assured him.

"Right," said Josh in Erie's body. "Gee, Jake, I mean Josh, I mean Jake. I don't know how to thank you."

"It's my pleasure," I said. "Now, go!"

I watched him jog back toward the trailer.

Then I looked down at the body I was now in. I hate to say it, but after being Erie Lake, Josh Hopka was a total letdown. One minute I was one of the most famous actors in the world. Next, I'm this slightly tubby, totally unknown kid. Life could sure throw some strange curves at you. But even in Josh's body, I had to smile. It would all be worth it to see Josh in Erie's body covered from head to toe with tarantulas.

As I started back across the parking lot I heard someone calling Josh's name, but I was so busy thinking about the tarantulas that I didn't remember whose body I was now in. A moment later Andy jogged up to me.

"Hey, Josh, didn't you hear me calling you?" he asked, panting for breath.

"Huh?" I gave him a puzzled look.

"Come on, Josh." Andy looked annoyed. "I must've called you five times."

"Oh, uh, sorry," I said in Josh's body.

"So, did you bring it?" Andy asked eagerly.

"Bring what?" I asked.

"The mini-DITS." Andy looked concerned. "Gee, Josh, what's with you?"

"Oh, uh, yeah." I patted Josh's day pack. "It's right here."

"Great," Andy said. "So we'll wait until lunch and then we'll grab Jake in Erie and make the switch."

"Right," I said.

Across the parking lot, the door to Erie's trailer opened and Josh in Erie's body came out, wearing a robe.

"Look at that jerk," Andy snorted. "Pretending he's Erie Lake the movie star. Who does Jake Sherman think he is?"

Right now he thinks he's Josh Hopka, I thought.

Andy and I walked up to the gym entrance. A security guard stationed there held up his arm. "Sorry, they don't want any extras hanging around inside."

"What's the big deal?" Andy asked.

"It's some kind of secret surprise scene," the guard said.

Andy and I had to wait outside the gym.

"A secret surprise, huh?" Andy grumbled. "Just wait until Jake gets the surprise we're gonna give him at lunch."

"He won't have to wait that long," I mused.

"What?" Andy asked.

"Oh, er, nothing," I quickly said. "I was just thinking about how strange and surprising life can be sometimes."

Andy gave me in Josh's body a funny look. "If you say so, Josh."

We waited outside the gym. I could easily imagine the scene inside. Drew DeMille and all the technicians, Josh in Erie Lake's body and all those tarantulas . . .

Suddenly the gym door flew open and Josh in Erie's body dashed out in his robe.

"You guys gotta help me!" he cried when he saw Andy and me.

"Why? What's going on?" Andy asked.

"You won't believe what they want me to do!" Josh in Erie's body cried. "It's horrible!"

"Hey, you wanted to be a big star, Jake," Andy said, still thinking that I was in Erie's body.

"No, no, you've got it all wrong, Andy," Josh in Erie's body cried, then pointed at me in Josh's body. "Maybe Jake wanted to be a big star. I just wanted to see what it was like."

Andy looked very confused. "Why are you pointing at Josh and calling him Jake?"

Before Josh in Erie could explain, Rita Picky came through the door. "Erie, what is wrong with you? They're just tarantulas."

"Tarantulas?" Andy repeated.

"Just give me a second," Josh in Erie begged Rita. "I have to go back to my trailer."

Rita put her hands on her hips. "Okay, but hurry, Erie. Everyone's waiting."

Josh in Erie's body hurried into the trailer. Andy and I followed him. As soon as we were inside, Josh in Erie's body locked the door behind us. Then he turned to me in Josh. "Get out the mini-DITS, Jake. I'm getting out of this body right now."

"Why did you call him Jake?" Andy asked. "He's Josh."

133

Josh in Erie shook his head. "No, he's Jake."

Andy's jaw dropped. "Wait a minute! If Jake's now in Josh's body, who's in Erie's body?"

"I am," answered Josh in Erie's body.

"But who are *you*?" Andy asked.

"Josh," answered Josh in Erie's body.

"You already switched?" Andy asked, surprised.

"It's a long story," Josh in Erie said. "I promise I'll explain it later. But right now, I have to get out of this body."

"Because of the tarantula?" Andy asked.

"Not tarantula," Josh in Erie corrected him. "*Tarantulas*. Lots and lots of tarantulas. Hundreds of tarantulas. *Thousands* of tarantulas. And they're all supposed to be crawling on me. I mean on Erie Lake."

"Yuck." Andy made a face.

"You bet yuck," agreed Josh in Erie's body. Then he turned to me in his body. "I want my body back, Jake."

I shook my, I mean Josh's, head.

"You *have* to give me my body back!" Josh in Erie insisted.

"Sure," I said. "I'll give you *your* body back when I get *my* body back. But there's no way I'm going into Erie's body with that tarantula scene coming up."

Josh narrowed Erie's eyes at me. "You *knew*

about the tarantulas! That's why you tricked me into switching bodies with you."

"You were going to play the same trick on me at lunch," I countered.

"Give Josh his body back," Andy said to me. "You're the one who wanted to be the movie star. I guess you just have to take the bad with the good."

"Forget it," I said.

Rap! Rap! Someone banged on the trailer door. "Erie? Erie, come out! Everyone's waiting!"

"It's Rita," I said.

Josh in Erie's body turned pale. "Come on, Jake, you *have* to give me my body back. *Please!*"

"No." I crossed Josh's arms firmly.

Josh in Erie gave us a desperate look. "What am I gonna do?"

"Find Erie in my body and have him switch with you," I said. "Then he'll be in his body and you'll be in my body. Then you and I can switch and everything will back to normal."

Josh in Erie's body quickly looked out the trailer window. "But Rita's waiting outside and I don't see Erie in your body anywhere."

I looked out the window. Rita Picky was staring in. When she saw me in Josh's body and Andy in the trailer, her face hardened with anger. She hurried away toward the school entrance.

"Uh-oh, guys," I said. "I think we're in trouble."

37

Less than a minute later, Rita was back. She had Principal Blanco with her.

And I could tell by how she was waving her arms and complaining that she was really ticked.

Bang! Bang! Principal Blanco knocked on the trailer door.

"Open up in there!" he shouted. "Josh Hopka and Andy Kent, you are supposed to be in school today. There was no call for you to be extras in the movie. If you don't come out right now, you'll both be suspended!"

"What are we going to do?" Josh in Erie cringed.

"I don't know about you guys," Andy said, "but I'm going to school."

Josh in Erie's body turned to me in Josh's body. "What about you, Jake?"

I looked outside. Rita Picky was speaking into her walkie-talkie. Her forehead was wrinkled and she looked really harried. She said something to

Principal Blanco, then rushed back into the gym.

Suddenly I had an idea. I went to the trailer door and opened it.

Outside, Principal Blanco glared up at me in Josh's body. "You are in big trouble, Josh."

"I know, sir," I said in Josh's body. "But could you come in here for a moment?"

Principal Blanco hesitated. "Why?"

"Erie Lake would like to speak to you," I said.

Principal Blanco blinked. His eyes went wide. "Really?"

"Yes," I said in Josh's body. "He says it's very important."

38

Principal Blanco climbed into the trailer.

"Josh said you wanted to speak to me, Mr. Lake," he said when he saw Erie. He didn't know it was Josh in Erie's body.

"I did?" Josh in Erie said. Behind Blanco, I nodded Josh's head hard. "Oh, yes, that's right, Mr. Blanco. I did want to speak to you. You see, I, uh . . ."

Josh in Erie looked at me in Josh for help.

"Remember the time you and I switched bodies?" I said in Josh's body.

"How could I ever forget it, Josh?" Principal Blanco asked. "You practically ruined my career."

"Well, Erie was wondering if you'd like to switch bodies with him," I said in Josh's body.

"*What?*" Principal Blanco looked really confused. "Why?"

"Because, er — " In Josh's body I tried to come up with a reason, but I couldn't think of one. I desperately looked to Andy for help.

138

"Because," Andy said, "Erie is having a, er, an attack."

"What kind of attack?" Principal Blanco asked.

"A, er — " Andy looked back to me in Josh's body for help.

"A bad hair attack," Josh in Erie's body ad-libbed.

Principal Blanco stared at Josh in Erie's body. "I don't see anything wrong with your hair, Mr. Lake."

"Well, that's just it!" I said in Josh's body. "There *is* nothing wrong with his hair."

"It's just that I *feel* there's something wrong with it," said Josh in Erie's body.

"And no matter what anyone says, he can't escape that *feeling*," Andy stressed.

"And as long as he *feels* that way, he can't act," I added in Josh's body.

"But what does that have to do with me?" Principal Blanco asked.

"Uh, well, have *you* ever had a bad hair attack?" Andy asked.

"No," answered Principal Blanco.

"Then you're *perfect*!" I insisted in Josh's body. "You're the only one among us who both knows that we can switch bodies *and* has real acting experience."

"He does?" Now it was Andy's turn to look puzzled.

"He acted in college," I explained in Josh's body.

The lines in Principal Blanco's forehead creased. "How do *you* know that, Josh?"

"Uh, Jake told me," I said in Josh's body.

"Well, this is all academic," Principal Blanco said. "The machine that switches bodies is locked in Mr. Dirksen's lab."

Bang! Bang! Someone was banging on the trailer door again.

"Erie!" Rita Pickey shouted outside. *"Everyone's waiting! You must come out now!"*

There was no time to lose. I quickly got the mini-DITS out of Josh's day pack and gave a headset to Principal Blanco.

"What's this?" our principal asked.

"Just put it on!" I slipped the other headset onto Josh in Erie's head.

"Why? Am I going to listen to something?" Principal Blanco asked as he put on the headset.

"You bet." I pushed the button on the mini-DITS.

Whump!

39

After the switch, Josh in Principal Blanco's body and Blanco in Erie's body were both a little woozy. Andy and I quickly helped our principal in Erie's body toward the trailer door.

"But wait!" Blanco in Erie dug in his heels. "All I really did was strip down to my underwear onstage."

"Then you're perfect for this role," I said and pushed him out the door.

"Finally!" Rita cried as the door opened. From the window we watched as Rita grabbed Erie's hand and dragged him back into the school gym. Little did she know that she was really dragging Principal Blanco in Erie Lake's body.

Josh in Blanco's body slumped wearily into a chair. "I can't believe it worked."

"What if Blanco freaks out over the tarantulas the way Josh did?" Andy asked.

"Forget it," I said. "There's no way they're going to let him out of there. He's doing that scene even if they have to tie him down."

Just then the door to the trailer swung open and Erie Lake in my body climbed in. "What's going on?" he asked. "I just saw Rita dragging Jake in my body into the gym. He, I mean I, looked really out of it."

My friends and I glanced at each other. I was in Josh's body. Josh was in Principal Blanco's body. Only Andy was in his own body.

"Jake isn't in your body anymore," Andy informed him.

"What?" Erie in my body looked shocked. "Then *who* is?"

"I'll tell you," I said. "But you won't believe it."

40

By the time we finished explaining what had happened, Erie in my body was scratching my head.

"Let me make sure I have this right," he said. "Josh is in your principal's body, and Jake is in Josh's body, and your principal is in *my* body?"

"Right," my friends and I said.

"How can you be so sure that Principal Blanco will want to switch back into his own body?" Erie in my body asked. "What if he wants to stay in my body the way you did?"

"Believe me," I assured him. "After this scene he'll never, *ever* want to spend another minute in your body again."

We waited. After a while the trailer door opened. Rita and Pasha helped Principal Blanco in Erie's body inside. Blanco in Erie's body looked dazed and needed help walking.

"What happened?" asked Erie in my body.

"We're not sure," Rita answered. "We think

that maybe Erie's just exhausted." Then she stopped. "What are you kids doing in here?"

I pointed at Josh in Blanco's body. "Principal Blanco changed his mind and said we could stay here as long as we understood the educational value of acting."

Suddenly Rita's walkie-talkie crackled. "Rita! You better get back here! The tarantulas are all over the place!"

"Oh, Lord!" Rita groaned. She and Pasha quickly helped Principal Blanco in Erie's body into a chair. Then she turned to Josh in Principal Blanco's body.

"Principal Blanco," she said, "could I ask you a really big favor? Do you think you could keep an eye on Erie?"

"Piece of cake," Josh in Blanco replied.

Rita turned to Pasha. "Come on, Pasha, I'm going to need your help with the tarantulas."

She and Pasha hurried out of the trailer.

The rest of us crowded around our principal in Erie Lake's body. He was slumped in the chair, staring blankly at the floor, with his mouth hanging open.

"What's wrong with him?" Erie in my body asked.

"I think being completely covered with big, hairy tarantulas has sort of left him *disturbed*," I said in Josh's body.

144

"Oh, right. The big tarantula scene." Erie in my body remembered. "I understand."

"What do we do now?" asked Andy.

"I guess we should wait until your principal comes to his senses," suggested Erie in my body.

"No way," said Josh in Blanco's body. "You know what's going to happen when Blanco comes to his senses?"

"He's going to go totally ballistic," I replied in Josh's body.

"Better believe it," agreed Josh in Blanco. "If we're going to do any more switching, we better do it right now."

41

Whump! We switched Erie in my body with Blanco in Erie's body. Now Erie had his own body back, and Blanco was in my body.

Whump! We switched Josh in Blanco's body with me in Josh's body. Now Josh had his own body back, and I was in Blanco's body.

Whump! We switched Blanco in my body with me in his body. Now I had my body, and Blanco had his.

Even after the rest of us had recovered from the shock of switching bodies, Blanco was still slumped in the chair, looking dazed.

"What do we do now?" Andy asked.

I headed for the trailer door. "We get out of here fast!"

We'd just left the trailer when Rita Picky came out of the gym and hurried toward us. "Oh, Erie! I'm so glad you're okay again! There's one little part of the tarantula scene we have to reshoot. Can you do it?"

Erie Lake flashed his famous smile and swept the hair out of his eyes. "You bet, Rita, baby. Just give me one minute." He turned to me and shook my hand. "I want to thank you for giving my body back, Jake, *and* for getting me excited about acting again."

"Glad to help," I said. "And I'm sorry about not wanting to give your body back sooner."

Just then five girls rushed up and begged him for autographs.

Erie grinned. "Believe me, Jake, I know just how you feel."

42

That night I was sitting in the den watching TV when my mom and dad came in. They both looked worried.

"Jake, have you seen your sister?" Dad asked.

"We don't know where she is," Mom said. "She usually calls if she's going to be out past nine."

Just then the front door opened. Jessica stumbled in with a glazed look in her eyes. She was dressed in her favorite clothes.

"Are you okay, hon?" Dad asked.

Jessica blinked. She slowly bobbed her head up and down.

"Are you sure?" Mom asked. "Because you're not acting okay."

"Erie and I rode in the limo," Jessica said dreamily. "Then we went up in the jet. And Erie . . ." Her words trailed off.

"And Erie . . . what?" Dad asked.

"Erie . . . *held my hand*!" Jessica announced and then wandered up the stairs.

Dad shook his head. "I do not understand it."

Mom smiled. "I do."

Dad turned to me. "What about you, Jake. Do *you* understand it?"

"We're not *supposed* to understand it, Dad," I said. "It's a *girl thing*."

43

They filmed in the school gym for another week. Each day the crowd of girls waiting to see Erie Lake grew smaller and smaller. By the time they finished shooting the locker room scenes, hardly anyone from school was there to see it.

One afternoon, Josh, Andy, and I were shooting baskets in my driveway.

"I saw Amanda Gluck today," Andy said. "She finally washed Erie's name off her forehead."

"Yeah, but I heard she went to a professional photographer and had her portrait taken first," Josh said.

"With his name on her forehead?" I asked.

"Better believe it," Josh said.

"Hey, look," said Andy.

Down at the bottom of my driveway, the long white limo pulled up and Erie got out.

"Hey, dudes!" Erie walked up the driveway and gave us all high fives. We gave him the ball, and he took a couple of shots. They were all swishes. Nothing but air.

"That reminds me," I said. "You never told us how you got so good at basketball."

Erie brushed the hair out of his eyes. "A couple of L.A. Lakers share the beach house next to mine. They've showed me a few moves."

"Got time for a little two-on-two?" Josh asked.

Erie shook his head. "Sorry, guys. Gotta fly back to L.A. We start filming the haunted house scenes tomorrow. I just wanted to stop and say good-bye."

We all shook hands and said so long. Then Erie started back down the driveway toward the limo.

"Hey, Erie," Andy called after him.

"Yeah?" Erie stopped.

"Would you ever do a movie about switching bodies with regular kids like us?" he asked.

Erie Lake thought about it for a minute, then shook his head. "Naw, guys, I don't think I could."

"Why not?" I asked.

Erie flashed his famous smile. "Because no one would believe it."

ABOUT THE AUTHOR

Todd Strasser has written many award-winning novels for young and teenage readers. Among his best-known books are *Help! I'm Trapped in Obedience School* and *Abe Lincoln for Class President*. His most recent books for Scholastic are *Help! I'm Trapped in My Camp Counselor's Body* and *Help! I'm Trapped in My Principal's Body*.

Todd speaks frequently at schools about the craft of writing and conducts writing workshops for young people. He and his family live outside New York City with their yellow Labrador retriever, Mac.

You can find out more about Todd and his books at http://www.toddstrasser.com